Frederick Edward Gould Lambart Cavan

With the Yacht and Camera in Eastern Waters

Frederick Edward Gould Lambart Cavan

With the Yacht and Camera in Eastern Waters

ISBN/EAN: 9783337412586

Printed in Europe, USA, Canada, Australia, Japan

Cover: Foto ©Andreas Hilbeck / pixelio.de

More available books at **www.hansebooks.com**

WITH THE

YACHT AND CAMERA

IN

EASTERN WATERS.

EARL OF CAVAN, K.P.

LONDON

SAMPSON LOW, MARSTON & COMPANY

LIMITED

St. Dunstan's House

FETTER LANE, FLEET STREET, E.C.

1897.

PREFACE.

BOTH my critics and the general public have agreeably surprised me. Of the thirty-five newspapers which kindly noticed my first book,* thirty-three were so friendly in their comments, that the most exacting Author could not wish more ; while the public have shown their appreciation in a very practical manner. I now venture a second work, in the hope that my readers may feel an equal interest in the places I have since visited, the photographs here given, and the short descriptions of those harbours which accompany the pictures taken.

In my last book there were a few printer's errors, which, I fear, gave my readers some slight annoyance ; my annoyance was very considerable. As for example, when so well known a Cape as "Spartivento" was spelt "Sparlivento," and even a better known locality, "Salerno," was spelt "Salermo." I must also, in this place, alter a passage, which *was* correct when it was written, but which is now incorrect. I alluded, in that work, to an incident which I spoke of as happening at Palermo, when three of my crew were unjustly fined for supposed smuggling. I then said, "the fines imposed were never returned." Just after my book was in

---

* "With the Yacht, Camera, and Cycle in the Mediterranean."

print, and six months after the event, I received the money back from our Foreign Office, which the Government at Rome had ordered to be returned to me. The greatest possible care has now been taken in the production of this book, and I sincerely hope that no errors may creep in.

I have a word of apology to offer to my tourist readers, who may be inclined to think that I have divided my book into too many chapters. As a matter of experience, I have found that on board every yacht, the guests invariably bring with them a large number of books to read, as they are likely, they think, to have much time on their hands. They certainly have plenty of time, but, as a rule they read very little, the truth of the matter being, that there are so many passing interests on board every vessel, that continuous reading is very difficult.

Of course, there are some exceptions. I have a friend, exceedingly well known in the scientific world, and equally well known in financial circles and in the House of Commons, who *never* has a book out of his hands. I verily believe he sleeps with one. Yet he is the most charming of all possible companions, for he tells you that he *can*, and very often *does*, take his attention off his book, and give all his attention to others without any inconvenience, so you may go and talk to him when you like, and he is delighted. But who is to write books for these exceptionally endowed people? No, I write for the ordinary yachtsman and tourist. He wants to take up his book readily and put it down easily; so, for him, short chapters. Also, to thoroughly understand what he is reading about, he likes a true picture before him of the places described, so photographs of these localities are a necessity; I have tried to oblige. I could have wished, for every reason, that we had been favoured with better weather during our Eastern cruise, chiefly because, owing to its badness, I have been compelled seriously to curtail the number of photographs I had hoped to offer, several pictures not having come out sufficiently well to publish; there were no less than 110 of these. While some of the selected ones, which I have given, are hardly as clear as I should have desired. Many others I have been more fortunate with, having watched for and secured favourable glimpses of light, and that light just coming at the right moment when I wanted it.

In regard to the encouragement given me to persevere in my desire to lay the whole Mediterranean before my readers, by means of photos and short descriptions, I certainly owe my best thanks to Commodore H.R.H. the Prince of Wales, for the kindly interest he took in my first work, and the special permission he gave me to dedicate that work to him.

Thanks are also due to many friends who, in a variety of ways, have given me their help, both in obtaining photographs and assisting me generally in my work. Amongst these, I should like specially to mention Major Edgar Lambart, R.A., and Mrs. Lambart, Mr. Maxse (British Consul at the Piræus) and Mrs. Maxse, who all aided me with their most kind and generous assistance. In my literary work, I further got many useful hints from Mr. Egerton (British Minister at Athens), Mrs. Egerton (née Princess Lobanoff), and Mr. Cecil Smith (the head of the British School at Athens).

To the authors of other guide books, whose works were of service to me before, I am again indebted.

In the appendix, at the end, I have drawn special attention to a scheme for improving the harbour in the Piræus, and I have given extracts from the *Field* newspaper, bearing upon the revival of the Olympian Games at Athens, which sports, if continued year after year, will form a very considerable attraction for both yachtsmen and tourists.

I feel that I am but a pioneer in the work I have undertaken, and the work of no pioneer can be said to be perfect; so my reader, though unable, possibly, to give unqualified praise to my efforts will, nevertheless, I hope, realize that a fresh departure in guide books has been made, and he may, possibly, be disposed to admit that, these endeavours are not without some value.

"ROSENEATH."

CONTENTS.

(xii.)

CHAPTER VII.

(xiii.)

CHAPTER XIII.

CHAPTER XIV.

CHAPTER XV.

CHAPTER XVI.

CHAPTER XVII.

APPENDIX.

ILLUSTRATIONS.

ITALIAN PROVISION BOAT.

CHAPTER I.

HAT is the twelfth to the Scotch Sportsman and the first to the English Sportsman? The months are too well known to require naming. Surely they are the dates most dear to their souls. The Yachtsman and the tourists have theirs also. They measure the whole year round, either from or to the dates they each fix upon to spread their wings and take their annual flight. To the man who not only owns, but commands and navigates his own vessel, this date means, or should mean, the satisfactory conclusion of a task which is always a labour of love; for fitting out, if it has its trials, has also its reward. Finding a crew, fitting out, provisioning, coaling and watering; these, in due course, are completed; now chose a suitable companion or companions; and your trip has begun. You meet your friends at some rendezvous, and the mutual greetings which pass between you are all *very* cordial ones. If they should not be, the result would soon show itself, for you *must* be together for months to come. On the present occasion I have only one companion to commence the trip with, though others are coming later.

I will not trouble my reader with the details of our outward journey from London to Leghorn, but will ask him mentally to accompany us on board the *Roseneath*, while together we make what I hope will prove a pleasant trip amongst the Greek Islands, and onwards to Constantinople. Charlie is our companion. He is wholly ignorant of the sea and and the ways of seamen ; he will soon learn. He is to do the photographic work for us, unless too ill. Will he be ?

We start from Leghorn October 6th; our ship's company consist of an English first mate, a Russian engineer, an English steward and valet, one Greek fireman, and the rest Italians; a mixed lot, no doubt, but certainly good men and true. Sober are they *always*, and willing ; but smart ? Well, they will improve, for they are hard working, and more than anxious to please. I need not describe the yacht and her equipment further, for I have given a photo of her, and further information may be obtained from Lloyds' Yacht Register, should the reader feel interested.

It was lovely weather when we left Leghorn, so with a fair breeze, and under easy steam, we sailed pleasantly during the day and anchored at Port Longone, in the Island of Elba, in the evening. A strong southerly gale sprang up almost at the moment we had anchored, and the harbour was soon well filled with small craft anxious to get shelter. During the night it blew hard, and at sunrise harder still. About 10 a.m. the largest water-spout I have ever seen crossed the mouth of

LEGHORN HARBOUR, INNER BASIN.

the harbour. It seemed quite a quarter of a mile broad ; fortunately it did no damage. Charlie and myself went early that day to visit Napoleon's house, and we photographed the grounds and the approach. It was a six mile drive from our anchorage. If you will look at the map, you will see that Port Ferrajo looks more sheltered from the prevailing winds than Port Longone, while it is certainly nearer Napoleon's house. Still, for some reasons, I preferred the latter port, for I was in want of neither coal or water, both of which can, no doubt, be more easily got at Port Ferrajo, but I fancy our port is, on the whole, better sheltered.

I do not think that any man, unless interested in the iron trade, would care for any lengthened stay in Elba. When you have seen Napoleon's bed and his study, and have looked out of the window he looked out of, and have tried to realize what he must have felt in exile, and how he arranged his clever escape, you will look for " other fields and pastures new," for there is nothing else here of interest. Grapes in plenty are grown on the Island, producing wines of good quality, excellent in taste and very rich in iron, but, when you are asked to try them, you will discover that they are sadly lacking in age. There is no one, perhaps, in Elba Island who would buy old wine, but there is cellar room enough in Ferrajo, under the houses, to store any quantity, and I feel sure it would pay for keeping, bottling, and exporting.

CHAPTER II.

E returned in the evening, after visiting the Emperor's house, and meant to sail next day. The weather, however, prevented us, and we passed a useless time watching for a lull, which was not forthcoming till 24 hours later. This we took advantage of, and, with fairly good weather, anchored off St. Stefano in the evening.

Here you may shelter in safety, and on either side of the promontory on which the lighthouse stands, according to the wind, and, if your vessel draws less than 15 ft., and you anchor well inshore, you may defy any gale that blows. The Admiralty chart last issued will give you all the soundings, and, at a glance, you will see how near to the land you may anchor. I hope it may not be out of place here, to remind my reader that the instructions given in the "Mediterranean Pilot" are drawn up, and most properly so, for sailing vessels. If you have steam, a good Captain, and a good leadsman, you can approach very close to the shore with absolute safety.

From St. Stefano, we sailed to Civita Vecchia, of which port I have given a description in my former

GAETA CATHEDRAL.

GAETA ANCHORAGE.

H.M.S. "CRUISER" LEAVING CORFU.

work,* and from thence to Gaeta, where we found
a fleet of Italian men-of-war at anchor. Here the
last Queen of Naples (a grand and noble woman),
did heroic deeds in defence of a hopeless cause. It
was not *her* fault that the Neapolitan Government
of that day was then what Turkish Government is
to-day. Need I describe it.

For courtesy and kindness, Italian naval officers
are hard to beat. We found it so here. For smart-
ness and utility the palm will, I fancy, be conceded
to the English. I could give details, but I write to
please, and would not, for the world, write a line
disparaging our charming allies and friends. This,
however, I can say, that as an *auxillary* force they
would prove of valuable assistance to any first-class
naval power. A glance at the splendid fleet anchored
here made me feel glad that England and Italy had
so much in common.

We sailed at daylight next morning, and anchored
off Santa Lucia harbour in the evening. I will not
weary my reader with an account of our easy and
pleasant voyage down the coast, anchoring first at
Santa Venere, and the next day at Messina, as in
the book before alluded to I have given short descriptions and photographs of these places, as well
as Corfu. At this last port we arrived on October
24th. We found H.M.S. *Cruiser* (training ship) at
anchor here. She went to sea daily, and it was a
grand sight each morning to watch her getting under
weigh. We remained for about a fortnight, and

---

* "With the Yacht, Camera, and Cycle in the Mediterranean."
Sampson, Marston & Low.

tried our luck on the Albanian coast. We shot a few pigeons, but the woodcock had not yet arrived, and with the pig we were unlucky. We found only two or three, and these we could not get at.

On November 3rd, we were joined by an old parliamentary friend of mine, who, for brevity, I will call Arnold. After he had joined, we tried our luck again, but Minerva had the sulks, and would neither throw her shield over us in the shape of a cloud, which, as the sun was shining hotly, would have been most welcome, nor recognise us as true sportsmen, so we were not favoured with success. Disappointing, of course. Our programme, however, was extensive, and we sailed for Guyo harbour, in the Island of Paxo* the next day (November 12th,) and for Ithaca* on the 13th. Could anything look more lovely than the harbour of Vathy as we entered? We *ought* all of us to have enjoyed it. I was the only one of the three on board, however, who could enjoy it at all.—Why? At dinner the previous evening we had all eaten fish; fresh, apparently, but indigestable. Arnold was really ill and prostrate; Charlie was slowly getting over it; while I, having eaten less than the other two, had recovered. Memo. —Mind you don't eat fish in the Mediterranean, unless you are absolutely sure that they have been caught well out at sea, not *inside* your port.

---

* See " With Yacht, Camera, and Cycle in the Mediterranean." Samson, Marston & Low.

GUYO, ISLAND OF PANO.

VATHY HARBOUR, ITHACA.

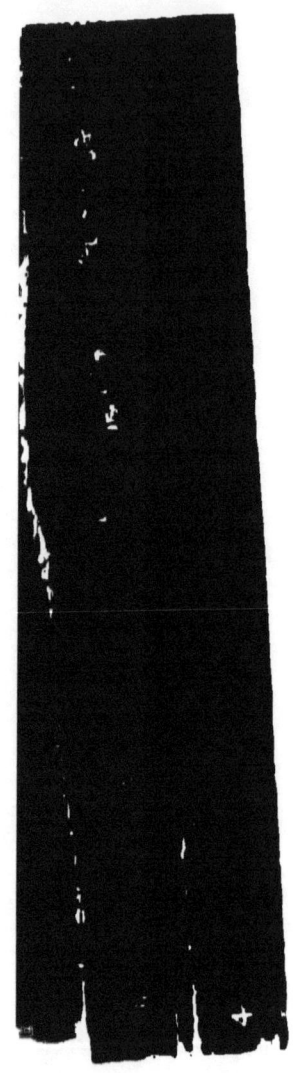

ARGOSTOLI, CEPHALONIA.

CHAPTER III.

EXT morning expeditions were formed to
see the Castle of Ulysses, and other
points of classical interest. We saw the
fountain of Arethusa, by the pleasant process of steaming round to it, and walking up hill about
one-third of a mile. Having collected some flowers
growing near, we returned on board, and steamed off
to Cephalonia. I selected the port of Argolstoli as
the best to anchor in. Here we remained for a few
days. The resident Vice-Consul was most kind, and
gave us some wines and brandy to taste, which were
home made so to speak, by a relation of his who
resides here. This enterprising English gentleman
certainly deserves success. I can very distinctly recommend the older wines, and the brandy, although now
only five or six years old, shows promise of becoming
one of choicest quality. It is absolutely pure and
unadulterated. There are lovely drives round about
the harbour and the neighbourhood. The hire price
of a pair of horses and carriage for the afternoon will
not reach 6s. The water here can be recommended
as pure and good; coal can also be got, but, of
course, before buying you must make your own
bargain. I know nothing more trying than the

realization of the fact that there is no fixed price for
ordinary goods in these parts. The time lost in
negociating a purchase is always trying, but I suppose
in some mysterious way, which I do not understand,
it is good for one. It is, anyhow, as complete a trial
of patience as could be experienced.

A gale kept us in Cephalonia a day longer than we
wished, but on the morning of Monday, November
18th, it moderated, and we sailed for Patras the next
morning, arriving at our destination that evening.
My good old friend, Mr. Wood (the Consul), was
delighted to see us, and showed my guests all the
chief places of interest in the neighbourhood. I
have described some of them in a former work, but
I should like to add, that a German firm, now established for some years, have been slowly developing
an extensive wine business, which promises well.
Our Consul can give information on this subject to
admirers of Greek wines and brandies. We all
passed a pleasant afternoon at the Consul's house,
while a game of lawn tennis, with real English balls
and our own rackets, put us all in a high glow and
good spirits. Exercise is the yachtsman's great
want, and a tennis court is a God-send after a long
stay on board ship.

The best of friends must part, and, after a two
day's stay, we bid adieu to our host and his family
who had all shown us great kindness. We then
proceed under steam to Itiar. Neither of my guests
had seen Delphos, so, on our arrival in the evening,
we make arrangements to take a carriage on the
next day up to the ruins. Business on board

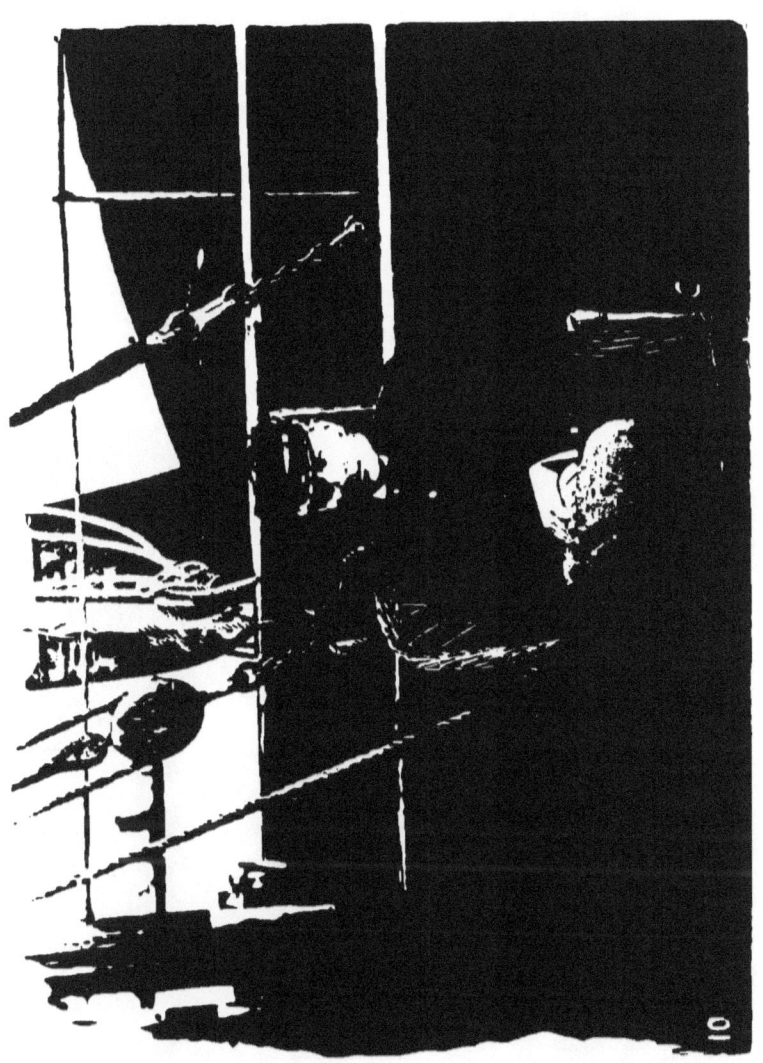

"ANXIOUS ABOUT THE POST."

"ALL RIGHT NOW."

prevented my accompanying them. They, however, started early, and spent a pleasant day examining the temple of Apollo, the museum, and other places of interest. A French guide very courteously showed them the newest excavations, and refused all recompense. I note this incident as at once rare and remarkable. From the description given by Arnold and Charlie, much work must have been done since my visit last spring, and visitors now may expect a real treat when tempted to undertake the excursion. It is useless to give less than a whole day to the visit. The roads, which I described in my last work, and which I found very bad, have been repaired, and a comfortable carriage, with three good horses, can now be engaged to bring you to the site of the ruins, after a pleasant drive of 2½ hours, while 1½ hours will suffice to carry you home again, and at a good pace, for your return journey is all down hill.

CHAPTER IV.

T came on to blow next day, as it very often will in these parts, and with very short notice, so I had some doubts whether it would be possible to put out to sea. The following morning, however, it moderated a little, though still blowing fresh, and we passed through the Corinth Canal after a patient wait of 1½ hours at the entrance. When the Canal is clear, the guide-books inform you that the red flag is hoisted. This *should* be so, but there are times when the officials forget their duties; so read your instructions, please, with a margin. Having, however, once passed through this interesting cutting, nothing but kindness and courtesy meet us. We wanted a few tons of water, so the Canal Company very generously supplied us, and with their own boat, immediately. I can only repeat what I have mentioned in my former book, as regards the badness of the water in the Piræus; so my reader will forgive me, if again I remind him of the necessity of coming in to that anchorage with a supply of good water on board. At Patras, if he is coming from the West, and at Poros, if he is coming from the East, he will find really excellent water which is inexpensively supplied. Having ourselves filled up the tanks at the mouth of the Corinth

ENTRANCE CORINTH CANAL, W. ENTRANCE.

RUINS NEAR ATHENS.

Canal, we sailed early next morning for the Piræus, arriving there in the middle of the day. Good fortune awaits us; my old friend, Mr. Stuart (late British Vice-Consul) was still here, and, placing ourselves in his hands, as regards coal, provisions, engineer's and ship's stores, we were as well and as reasonably provided for as could be desired. To meet a really honest and trustworthy man in these parts, who will further take the trouble to see himself that you are well served, is a piece of good fortune we thoroughly appreciated. Three Austrian men-of-war, one Greek ironclad, and a Russian cruiser, are at anchor inside the harbour, also an American vessel just outside; they all remind us of that ever present Eastern question which has just now come so prominently to the front. At all dinner tables and parties where Ministers and Diplomatists meet, every one is talking of the Conference to be held at Constantinople. Will it succeed for a few more years in patching up the *status quo*, or is the climax near? Who knows, or can know, when the nations which send representatives cannot tell themselves what fresh outbreaks or troubles may arise. These would complicate the already difficult position four-fold.

At Athens we are now more than ever interested in the British* School of Archæology, which, since last year, has been enabled to make a fresh start under the able superintendence of Mr. Cecil Smith, of British Museum fame. Since last year, a sum of

---

* See page 31 of "With Yacht, Camera, and Cycle in the Mediterranean," Sampson Marston & Low.

£500 a year has been granted by the Government for five years, towards the expenses of the school. Should it prove a success, there is little doubt but that a further extension will be applied for, and possibly granted. I hope my readers will not think me prolix in calling attention to our school, for every yachtsman, tourist, and student will find this Institution of real use to him. My friend, Mr. C. Smith, is always pleased to give valuable information in regard to the excavations now being made, and any student may take my word for it that a short period passed in the School Library will amply repay him.

On Saturday, November 30th, Arnold leaves us to go on by steamer to Constantinople, and thence home. We all miss him, but no one more than the writer. He is one of the few men one meets who can really talk well. I have listened to him night after night, and always regretted the arrival of the hour when it was time to go to bed. The British Consul and Mrs. Maxse came on board, Thursday, December 5th, and we sailed for Poros Harbour, 28 miles from the Piræus. A more beautiful anchorage I have never seen. Our lady guest is a true artist, and takes a fresh sketch on each of the five successive days we remain here. Bad weather and gales all the time. The holding ground is good, and the best water conceivable can easily be obtained. We thoroughly appreciate this last blessing, as the Piræus water is as bad as possible. Yachtsmen and tourists beware. Before leaving, Mr. Maxse (a really first-class photographer) and Charlie get some photos of the place.

MRS. MANSE, OWNER, AND CREW OF "ROSENEATH," POROS, 1895.

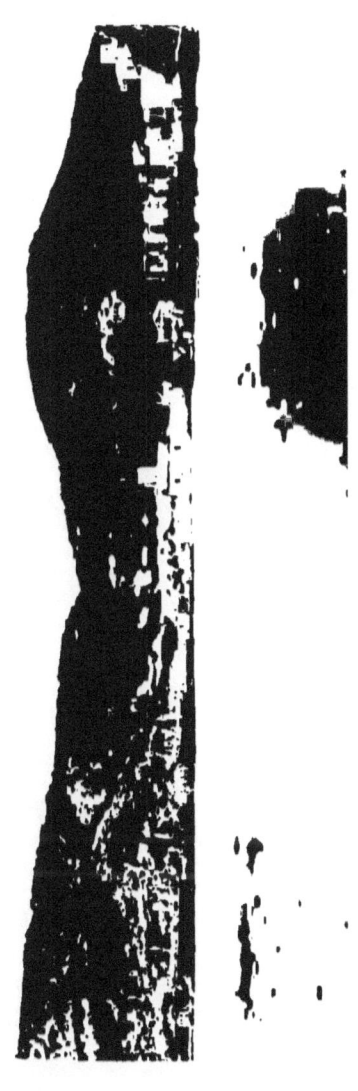

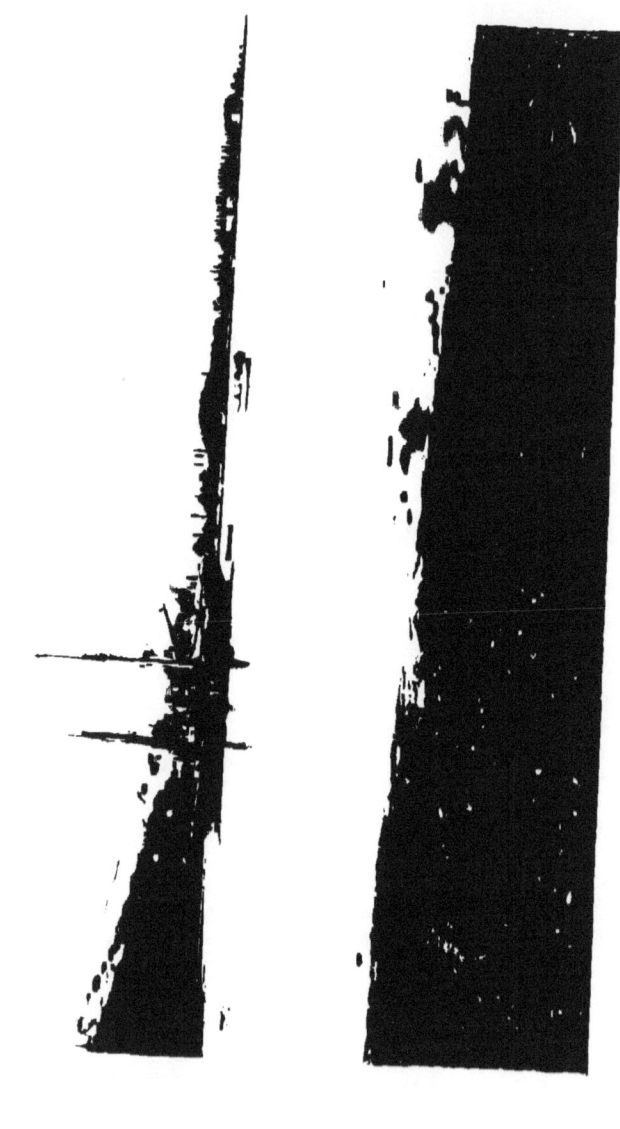

CHAPTER V.

N Wednesday, December 11th, we leave Poros Harbour, the weather having greatly improved. I have been much struck by the warning which the glass invariably gives of coming bad and good weather. There really is little excuse to be made for any Captain who neglects its warning. On December 13th, a falling glass indicates that a breeze is coming. During the next three days it blew a whole gale.

From our anchorage we could see the sea outside, and a more angry one I have never observed, except in the North Sea. The Piræus was soon crowded with vessels of all sorts. The harbourmaster must have had a hard time of it. On the 14th, the gale still continued. The 15th (Sunday) promised better weather.

Herbert (another friend of mine) joined us in the evening and reported very bad weather in the Adriatic. He had come straight out from England, *via* Brindisi.

Monday 16th, we shifted our berth. It took us all day to clear our anchors; a large merchant steamer having fouled them. We anchored, eventually in the evening, near the King's Yacht, and in a good berth.

Thursday 17th, Captain Douglas, who had been with me for 18 months, left to go home for private reasons. I engaged a pilot in his place, who had some experience of the Dardanelles. My friend came on board in the evening to dinner, having seen more of Athens in two days than most men do in a week. Very active is Herbert.

Wednesday, December 18th, we crossed over to the comfortable harbour of Poros, and, having got our water on board early the next morning, we sailed mid-day for Zea Island, arriving at Port St. Nikolo in the afternoon about 2 p.m. The barometer was high during the whole of these two days, though, curiously enough, the sky kept threatening. My pilot remarks that "it would blow and rain too, if it was not for the glass." My own view of the case was that it blew quite hard enough as we crossed over, though the rain still kept off. Port St. Nikolo is the place where the "Royal Albert," one of our old three-deckers, was beached about 40 years ago, as, owing to an accident to her screw shaft, she was leaking badly, and was only saved from sinking by this means.*

Friday, December 20th, we sailed from this charming little port. The glass still continuing to fall during the night, I hoisted my boats in and lowered the topmasts. Overhead and all round it looked as peaceful and calm as could be wished, but we are near the shortest day, and tradition has it, that on and near that day storms are to be looked for in these parts. At 2.30, we anchored at Mykonos, in

---

* See " Murray's Guide to the Mediterranean," Vol. I., page 151.

HERBERT.

PORT ST. NICOLO, GULF OF ATHENS.

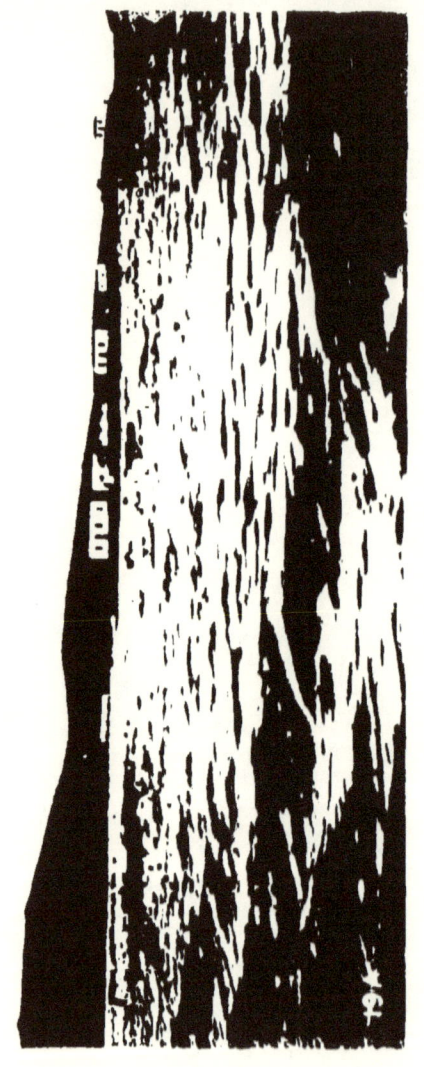

DELOS ANCHORAGE.

the Korpho, off the mole in 13 fathoms, the wind
having increased. There is a really good anchorage
here, and to the antiquarian there is much which is
interesting to see and even to hunt for, as tradition
tells both of temples and statues yet undiscovered.
Delos is only three miles off; which we remember
was the birth-place of Apollo and Artemis. It was
considered *the* Holy Island, principally, no doubt, on
account of the oracle which in sanctity was only
second to that of Delphos. Necessity has compelled
us very unwillingly on this occasion to pass by the
Island of Syra. We looked from the distance on to
its prosperous town with its 26,000 inhabitants and
its splendid harbour, and promised ourselves a nearer
acquaintance on our return journey from Constantinople. Report speaks very highly of the health as
well as the wealth of its inhabitants. It must have
been a surpassingly lovely place when covered with
trees, of which, alas, not many remain. We had
hoped the glass would not continue to fall, but it did,
so we gave up the idea of leaving shelter, and on
December 21st, as we had steam up, we ran across
under the lee of the islands to Delos, anchoring off
the Custom House in eight fathoms. So clear was
the water that we could easily see our anchor.
About 3 p.m., a very heavy squall struck the yacht,
but we had a second anchor ready which we let go,
and, having plenty of sea room, veered on both
cables and rode out the gale in great comfort.

December 22nd, Sunday. The shortest day in the
year has arrived and we have turned that corner.
The glass in the morning began to rise. It was still

very low, so I determined to remain one more day at anchor and give the sea a chance to go down. In the middle of the day Herbert, the pilot, and myself crossed over to Old Delos to examine the ruins. The Grotto from whence the Oracle was supposed to speak, was in fairly good repair, but the temple of the foreign gods, the temple of Apollo, as well as the temple of Latona, were all in a hopeless confusion of ruin. The site of the Stadium, however, though its marble seats were scattered and broken up, could easily be made out, and a fair idea of its ancient magnificence is suggested to the mind as one stands on the South side of it. The same may be said of the Theatre. What I think struck us most were four mosaic pavements in houses adjoining the Temples. These remained absolutely intact, the colours looking as bright as if they were new. It is now about 2,000 years since they were placed in position.

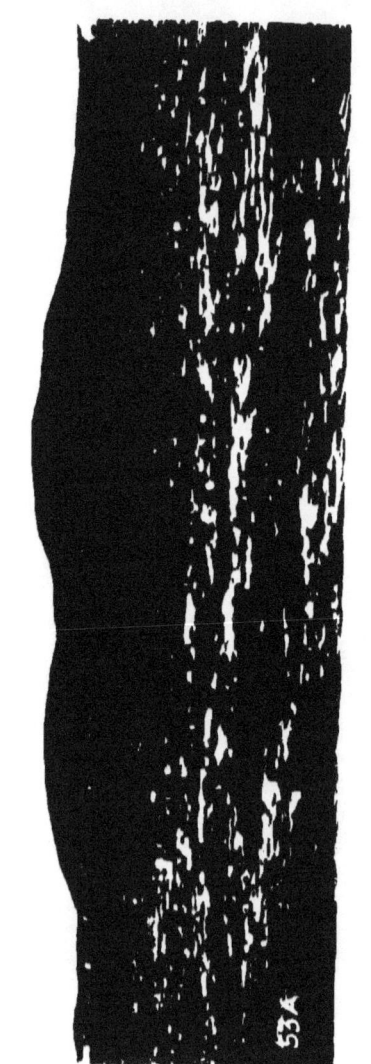

ARSIDA ISLAND, GULF OF ATHENS.

CHAPTER VI.

N Monday, 23rd, at 2 p.m., I tried to sail across to Chios, but the wind and the sea were too boisterous when we were fairly outside and clear of the Islands to proceed. I, therefore, hove to under the lee of the land till daybreak, and then, having put in to Syra for provisions, I returned to our old anchorage in Delos. Syra was, not many years ago, a most flourishing town; this was in the days of the old wooden ships. Now the trade has decreased, and, though new leather works and one or two warehouses partially cover the ground where once ship building yards stood, the population has decreased, and is decreasing. Here there is a British Consul.

By the vicissitudes to which places, like persons, are subject, Syra, though insignificant in former history, has, owing to its central position, become of late years a great emporium. The ancient Greek city stood on the site of the present town, close to the harbour; only a few fragments are left of foundations and walls. In the middle ages, the inhabitants retreated for security from pirates to the lofty hill, about a mile from the shore, on the summit of which they built the town, now called Old Syra.

C

18

The island was of no importance till the war of the Revolution. Then the immigration of refugees from different parts of Greece, especially from Chios and Psara, rapidly raised it to its present flourishing condition. Pherekydes, the instructor of Pythagoras, and himself one of the earliest among Greek philosophers to maintain the immortality of the soul, was a native of Syros.

The modern town, called Hermoupolis, contains upwards of 26,000 inhabitants. It is built round the harbour, on the East side of the island. A stately lighthouse, rising on a rock in front of the harbour, a quay with numerous warehouses, and several handsome houses, built of white marble, show the mercantile importance of the place; but the streets are still narrow and crooked, though clean and well paved. Vestiges have been found of the temples of Poseidon and Amphitrite. Great attention is here paid to education; there are more than 3,000 scholars in the various schools. The favourite promenade in the cool of the evening is on a cliff to the North of the town.

Old Syra is seated on the hill which commands the port, and is now so connected with the new town by continuous buildings, that the two may be regarded as one city. This hill, from its remarkable conical form, resembles a huge sugar loaf covered with houses. The ascent is very toilsome, up steep streets, crossed by a narrow flight of steps. On the top stands the church of St. George, from which the view is very fine; below may be seen the church of the Jesuits. Old Syra contains about 6,000

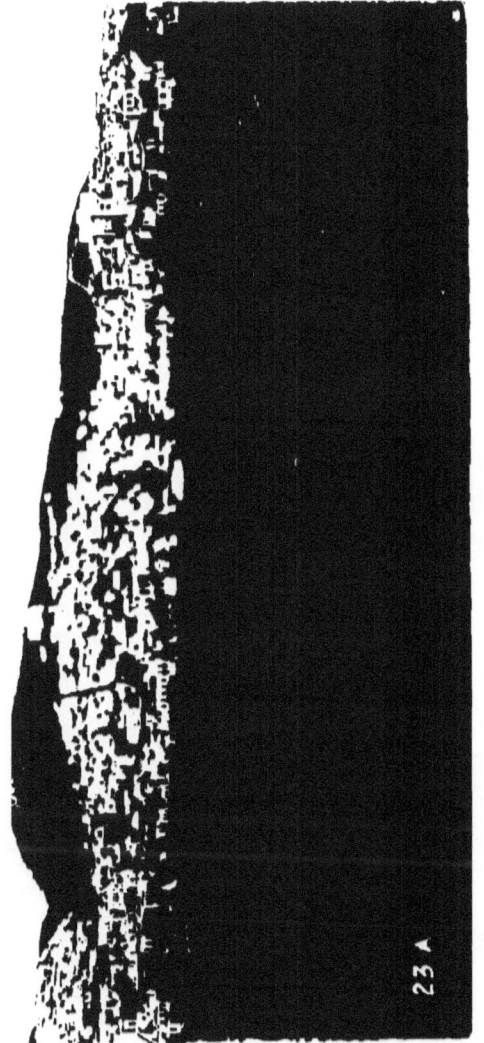

SYRA.

23

inhabitants, mostly Roman Catholics; often at variance with their Greek neighbours, who regard them as aliens. Generally speaking, the Roman Catholics of the Levant are descended from Genoese and Venetian settlers of the middle ages. They have always regarded themselves as under the protection of France; but the nationality of the Latins of Syra was the chief cause of the modern prosperity of the island, which became, during the Revolution, the refuge of numerous merchants from the distracted parts of Greece.

On Tuesday, December 24th, we sailed at 4 a.m. for Chios, with a fine light breeze on the starboard quarter, so that, under steam and sail, we covered the first 61 nautical miles in 6 hours. We arrived in the evening at Kastro. Here Herbert and myself landed, and were shown what there was to see by the General Manager of the English Telegraph Company. We owe our best thanks to him for his kindness and courtesy. There is not much of interest to attract except, perhaps, the new Greek church and Turkish Hospital (really a good one), but these will repay a visit. To telegraph anywhere to the Company's stations costs about 6d. a word, and this within the narrow limits of Greece and Turkey. The harbour is not a convenient one in any way, and the anchorage outside is not good. Yachtsmen be "off out of this," as our friends of the Emerald Isle would say, and as soon as you can. The only thing you will find here worth waiting for is water. For your coal go to Smyrna, if voyaging East, and to Syra if going West or South.

20

We left next morning, December 25th, eating our Christmas dinner at Smyrna. Coaling and watering occupied the crew next day, while Herbert and myself visited the Bazaar, in company with a guide very kindly provided for us by the Consul General. The strings of camels entering with goods, the dirt of the streets, and the extortionate demands of the shopkeepers, all remind us that we are no longer in Europe. As our time, on this occasion, is limited, we have not found it possible to make any of the interesting excursions to Ephesus and the neighbourhood, which every visitor here is expected to undertake. I have, however, some information for my yachting friends. If you want to enter the harbour, you must apply either to the harbour-master, or, better still, through the Consul General to the proper authorities for leave; this may take a day or two. In the meantime, there is a very good anchorage in about five or six fathoms 300 yards from the entrance of the harbour, and looking straight into it. This outer anchorage is so good, and the harbour is so dirty that, unless I had some important repairs to make or some very good reasons for entering, I would much prefer remaining outside. If you like to go about 600 yards from the entrance of the harbour, and about 120 to 140 yards from the shore, you will then be clear of the large steamers which come to the roadstead frequently, but do not enter the harbour. The only disadvantage you will suffer from is the distance your provision boats have to come before reaching you. I think another time, should I visit this port again, I would anchor

QUAY, SMYRNA.

pro. tem. as near the entrance of the harbour as they would allow me, just for coal and water, and then shift berth as I have suggested about 600 or 700 yards away. Both these can be obtained on your arrival. All your wants can (it is declared) be supplied by at least ten different persons, who, in as many boats, flock or board your vessel. My advice is, deal with *none* of them, but, calling on the Consul General, listen to what he has to say, or, better still, write privately to him beforehand. His courtesy, his great knowledge of the place, and his power to make himself useful, will fully repay you for the apparent delay. A more able and courteous official does not serve the Queen. Now to return. It can rain in Smyrna as well as elsewhere, and, as the more interesting newspapers are stopped here before they reach their destination, you had better give up all hope of getting news, and hunt up your library. Sight-seeing is impossible. There exists no term in our English language, I could place on paper, which adequately describes the state of the streets. Could the English Government, 3 years ago, have seen its way to assist in forming and opening the railway between Smyrna and Constantinople, a large trade would then have been opened out, and Smyrna would then have been enriched and improved in every respect. It is now too late ; and both France and Germany have acquired interests since, which should have been British.

On December 27th, we left for the small but perfect little harbour of Foujes or Foggia. It was a short sail of only 30 miles, but a windy one. Herbert and myself landed in the evening, and were much struck with the industrious aspect of the place, and the busy Greeks discharging or loading the small craft which ply with stores up and down the coast. Though a Turkish town, by far the larger portion of its inhabitants are Greeks.

December 28th, we sailed for the North Port of Mitylene. The South Port has only 3 fathoms of water in it, at its deepest part. The North has 4 or 5 in its deepest, and but 2 and 3 fathoms all round its centre. It is small and wholly unsuitable as a winter anchorage. From the North Point to N.E. it is wholly unprotected. We rode out a fearful gale here, with three anchors ahead and steam to help us in the heaviest squalls. A more miserable couple of days I have seldom spent. I never slept for more than $1\frac{1}{2}$ hours at a time during the whole gale, and was on deck always. Herbert was plucky in the extreme, but his sufferings must have been great, as he is by no means a perfect sailor. A more cheerful companion under adverse circumstances I cannot imagine, and when, on the afternoon of December 30th, the storm lulled and we could lower a boat, he went on shore and had a good walk, meeting on his road an Englishman, who was employed as an Engineer putting up some machinery for a Greek merchant. This gentleman gave him all the local news. If my brother yachtsmen will take my advice, they will not enter this harbour under any pretence whatsoever. In St. Paul's day, either he or the captain of his ship came to the sensible con-clusion that one day's stay was sufficient. I wish they

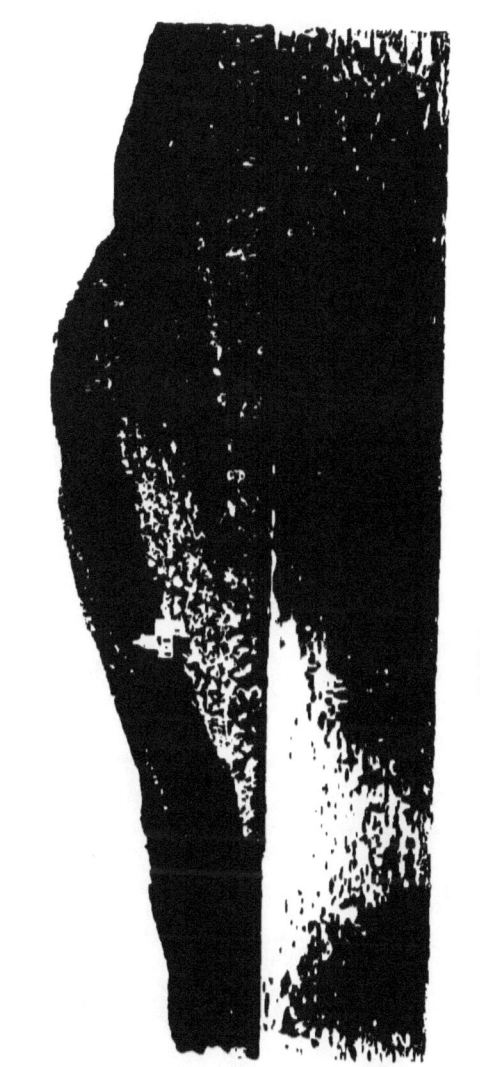

LIGHTHOUSE OFF FOGGIA.

had passed on their experiences. I do not, of course, allude to other anchorages in the Island, I only speak of the two ports on each side of the town of Mitylene. Jero, or Hero, harbour is, of course, magnificent, *when* you get into it, but the entrance is very narrow, *vide* " Mediterranean Pilot," vol. 4.

Chapter VII.

N December 31st, we sailed for Chanak in the Dardanelles, arriving there at 10 p.m. By some stupid mistake on the part of the Turkish garrison, who, for some unknown reason, fancied we were not going to anchor for the night, they first burnt a blue light and then fired two guns (unshotted), to warn us off. The next gun would have been shotted, and fired *at* us, so I took down our steam lights (a most improper proceeding) before we anchored. This satisfied them.

Next morning, January 1st, we got our pratique at Chanak, and proceeded for Gallipoli. Here we took in 9½ tons of water, for which a Greek charged us 5s. a ton, having made out his bill for 11 tons. Yachtsmen beware. To get this on board we had to go round to the North harbour, and only just got back again to the Southern anchorage in time to save being caught in one of the worst blizzards of sand and wind I have ever known. There is a strong current in the North harbour, especially during Northerly winds, and in steaming out of it great care is required while turning the ship to seaward. It blew a hurricane for two whole days and nights. The cold was so intense that we had to

keep the engine room door open to get warmth, while two Cera stoves in the saloon hardly kept us warmed. The yacht rolled about a good deal, and it was difficult to get any rest. We had both anchors down. It is worth while here to mention, that quite close into the mouth of the little port there is a depth of 4 fathoms; it is most advisable to anchor as close to this as possible. There is a current which swirls round the bay which causes a nasty sea to rise, and the closer in you can get the better for you. We dressed for dinner each evening, I will tell you how. First we put on all the warmest clothes we had, then fur coats over them, and warm rugs round our legs. In this way we got our dinner. Of course we used, indeed we could only use, swinging plates,* the ship was knocking about so much. The men (all Italians) were cheerful throughout, and when we weighed one anchor, which we did on the morning of January 3rd, they all worked as well and cheerfully as if to work in frost and snow was an every day affair with them. They deserve every praise. Herbert "fell in" to the capstan, and by kindly lending us a hand to get our anchor up, he got warm for the first time, he declared, for four days.

On January 1st, I forgot to mention that we called on the Vice-Consul, and found him in the midst of his family entertaining all his friends; five Consuls and Vice-Consuls were there. I had a long conversation with our hostess and the French Vice-Consul. They cannot see how war can be averted.

---

* My own Patent.

26

The news from England as regards the American difficulty was, however, good. We were most grateful for this.

The trade of Gallipoli is entirely in the hands of Greeks or Jews. The houses are built of wood. A fire here, with a high wind, would be most disastrous. To the tourist I would say, the town is *not* worth a visit; and to the yachtsman, come in here for shelter of course if it suits you, but get away as soon as you can. Game is cheap however, and it may be worth your while to lay in a stock. Woodcocks and hares, 1*s.* each; partridges, 1*s.* 6*d.* a brace. So buy what you want, and then go away. If, however, for any reason, you are delayed, you will find the Vice-Consul, and his charming wife, both pleasant and agreeable. They speak French and Italian. English is not spoken here at all, or very little.

January 4th, we weighed from Gallipoli, the gale having moderated, and came to an anchor again in Kutali roads at 3 p.m., the weather looking again most threatening. From North and North-Easterly gales these roads offered very convenient shelter; from the village itself some provisions can be obtained. We have now had three weeks of really bad weather, intense cold and adverse gales, only here and there a day when it was possible to go to sea. Water, and the best, can be got near Kutali in breakers, if required, and for every reason I strongly recommend this anchorage. That the prospect is dreary in the winter I do not deny, but those who look for warmth need not travel amongst the Turkish Islands during the inclement season.

GALLIPOLI (TURKEY) FROM ANCHORAGE, S. HARBOUR.

27

Early on the morning of January 5th, we weighed, and, with reefed main trysail, jib and staysail, assisted by steam, we made the best of our way through stormy rain, snow, and wind, to the roadstead anchorage on the South West side of St. Stephano Lighthouse. We just reached this before dark, and anchored in 6½ fathoms. The whole of the coast as far as Constantinople offers to the anxious Captain quiet shelter from all North and North Easterly gales, which in these parts should be regarded as recurring regularly every few days during the months of December and January. Constantinople is certainly worth a visit (my readers have heard this before), but if you are to come out in your yacht, or by one of the many steamers which run to the Bosphorus, you must pay for the luxury in endurance as well as in money. If you are the right side of sixty, and in good health, then come by sea; but if not, then go by rail. This is my advice. Of course I am now only speaking of the winter season. Things change wonderfully for the better in March, and the weather does not often get bad before the middle, or even the end of November. This year it was fair at Constantinople till about the second week in December, so I was told. I cannot imagine how any weather can be much worse than that which we have had, and without a break for the last fortnight, so beware of January.

Chapter VIII.

ANUARY 6th, we managed to get into Constantinople, and came to an anchor just in time to get Major and Mrs. Lambart on board, as we were preparing for the coming hurricane, the glass giving us warning. It came on that evening, and blew with all, if not more than its usual force. It continued with unabated fury for 4 days. Then cold with snow, then fairly fine. Constantinople is always interesting, and we make the best use we can of our time here. From the Ambassador downwards every one is kind. We note all the information we receive from our friends in general, but here, however, it is worth mentioning, that all reports and rumours which concern Turkey, and which one hears in the hotels and places of public resort, require scrutiny, for there is little reliance to be placed on the chatter of the place. In Constantinople there is no newspaper published which in England we should think worthy of the name. I believe this to be the general view.

The eyes of the diplomatic world are always more less directed in an Easterly direction. During the winter of 1895-96, the whole world has been engaged in studying the Turk and his ways, while

diplomacy seems to have exhausted its every
effort in an endeavour to solve the most puzzling
of problems. Constantinople every one knows. I
do not give photographs for two reasons. There is
too much smoke from the steamers to ensure good
pictures, and for navigating purposes photos would
be of no real value. There have been many pictures
given by illustrated papers. It is an immense City
as it is, but could it be peopled with English, French,
or Germans, it would more than double in size in less
than 10 years.

Its capacity as a trading port is inexhaustible.
Think of its many advantages. Here the purest
drinking water can easily be obtained in any quantity,
and also at small expense. An easier town to drain
does not exist, as, at the foot of the seven hills on
which it is built, runs a stream of salt water 1 mile
wide and 30 fathoms deep. This stream is running
always at the rate of from 1 to 4 miles an hour,
according to circumstances. Valleys, in which vege-
table produce and grain will grow for seven months
out of the year, abound in every direction, while
gentle slopes with a Southerly aspect can be relied
upon for about 8½ months. But a human curse is
over the land. Justice is bought, trade stagnates,
murder is common, theft universal. Honesty is a
sign of weakness. Thrift excites the jealousy of
every neighbour, and it is well if this is all. Woman
has her place in the land, and it could not be lower
or more degraded. Of course I speak generally, but
even here an exception exists, as if to prove the rule.
Take a walk, if you will, in Stamboul proper, and

even some parts of Galata, and you will see hard
working Turks, as well as Greeks, against whom but
one word can be said : "who would be free themselves must strike the blow." How true everywhere,
but nowhere more true than here. Where lies this
young Armenian's brother ? where the father of that
one ? and where the husband of that modest young
Armenian wife? But last year they lived: to-day
the Bosphorus or the neighbouring prison owns
them ! These are as good, or rather as bad, as dead.
At the massacre of the Armenians last year, hundreds
were killed, while the Sultan's spies have recently
carried off numbers of suspected persons, and once
inside those Turkish walls, then, indeed, farewell
to every hope.

I visited most of the places of interest in 1853, and
again in 1856, when a young midshipman. This was
just before and just after our Crimean campaign.
Things have changed but little since, and almost in
every respect for the worse. There are some exceptions, however. The museum is new and good.
Remains from the site of Troy, the reputed sarcophagus
of Alexander the Great, and a few other objects of
interest really repay a visit. The Ottoman Bank
buildings are fine and new. The Pera Hotels are
good; almost all of them. We visited the "Pera
Palace" Hotel and the "Bristol," and found them
excellent, but the drainage everywhere is bad; that
is, of course, as judged from a Paris or London
standpoint. The harbour is as badly regulated as
possible ; it might be (*after* Bizerta, of course), the
best harbour East of Gibraltar. The streets, except

one in Pera, are beyond doubt the worst in the world. I know the streets of Canton, so I speak from experience.

On January 10th, Friday, we went to the Yildiz Kiosk Palace, and saw the Sultan going to Mosque; 7,000 troops kept the ground. The men and some officers were fine looking, strong, and doubtless excellent soldiers. The Commanders, in appearance, I decline to say a word about, one only shall be mentioned,—Osman Pacha. *He* looked what he was, a soldier, and a brave one too. We went, after the ceremony, wishing to see the dancing Dervishes. Here we were to find enthusiasm, and really deep religious feeling, sympathize or not as we might. Alas! the principal dancing Dervish had caught a cold, so there was no dancing. The Mosque of St. Sophia, the remains of what was once the most interesting bazaar in the world, before the fire of 1870, and the walls of the old city, are in turn each visited.

From an eminence at Pera, we look over the Golden Horn. Here are laying at anchor 5 Turkish battleships and 5 coast protectors. They went to sea last in 1878. Their crews are 3,500 all told; these have yet to go to sea and learn their work. 15 torpedo boats and torpedo catchers are here also, 5 of these have been to sea. They were up to date in 1888. The army has many months pay due to it. The Constantinople force (about 7,000 men) being the only troops paid regularly; they guard the Sultan. Ball practice was ordered between 3 and 4 years ago for the last time; blank cartridge has been considered safe and sufficient since. The new Artillery Barracks are really splendid,—I think the finest pile of military buildings I have seen anywhere. A knowledge of how to use the field guns within its square is to follow, but at present this instruction remains in an embryo condition. Education and progress is not only required in naval and military matters, but by everyone in every department, and everywhere.

Herbert and myself are Liberals in England, here we are absolutely agreed with every Tory we meet. We all praise and blame the same people and the same institutions. Constantinople is so cut off from all progressive civilization, as that term is understood in England, France, or Germany, that there is no room for small differences. We go to the Club. The "Times" of two days ago was stopped altogether, to-day the middle sheet has been suppressed. We are allowed to read only what the Sultan and his officers consider good for us, so we are all reformers now, and thorough-going ones too. Our Ambassador here we call upon, in order to pay our respects. Of what sort is he? The best possible, but he has a superhuman task; he struggles quietly and manfully with it. His staff are, indeed, excellent, and work with a will to help their chief. They deserve the credit due to persons who are continually rolling a stone up hill. For them there is no down hill, no flat. Bigotry, fanaticism, ignorance, filth, and alas, failure must be the enemies most familiar to them, and against which they daily fight. Let us turn aside, this picture is too dreadful to contemplate. Here is a better—

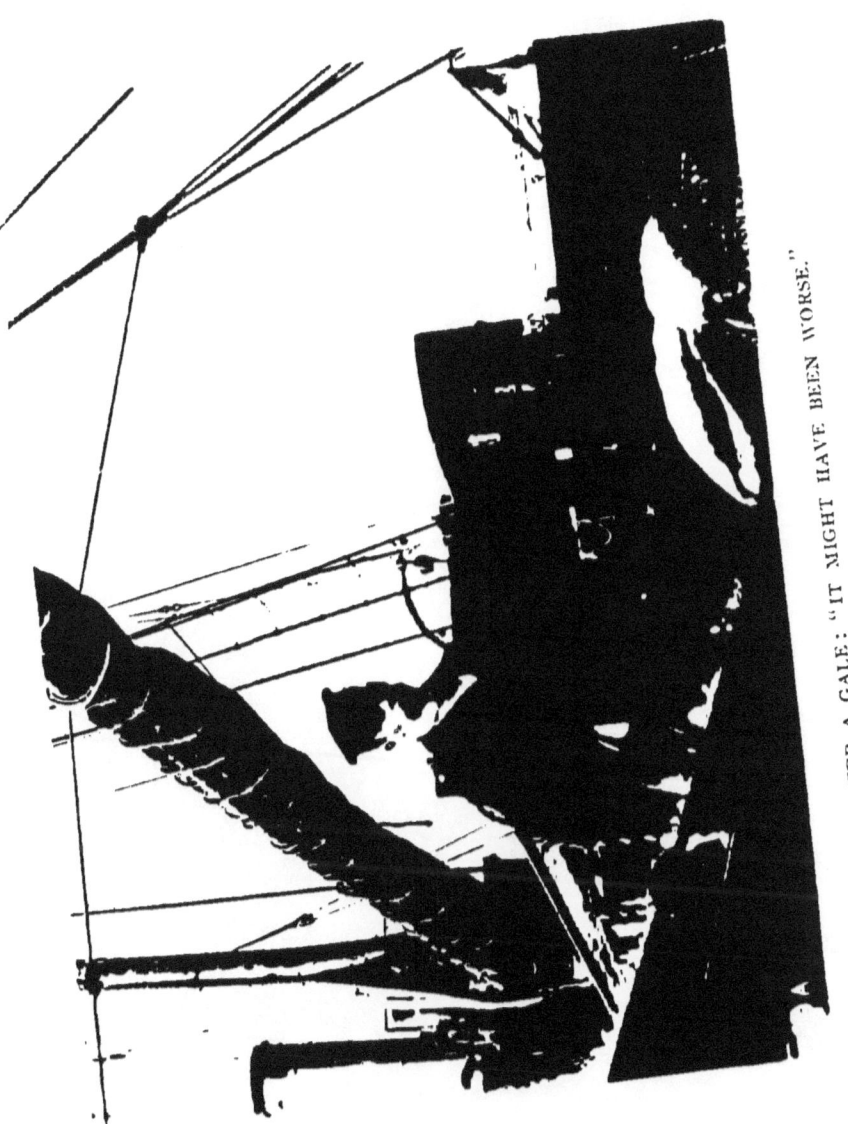

AFTER A GALE: "IT MIGHT HAVE BEEN WORSE."

33

The moon is shining on the Minarets, the Turkish part of the town is illuminated with many lamps ; Turkish ships, too, in the harbour, are lighted up, there is a calm, and it is not too cold to enjoy the sight. The day is January 11, a Mohammedan Festa. Feast your eyes patient traveller ; you have neither seen nor heard much to delight you before. News-papers there are here, no doubt, and in to-morrow's press the illuminations will be reported. This *will* be allowed by the authorities. The English press correspondents have their work cut out for them, and it is wonderful how accurate their reports are, considering the almost super-human difficulties they have to contend against, and then with what ability do they write. All the leading London newspapers have special correspondents at Pera, and Reuter's telegrams are forwarded by a gentleman whose local knowledge and daily information cannot be surpassed. How are things going on now ? In the "Standard" of January 2nd will be found a very accurate descrip-tion of the state of the country round Stamboul, and those who care to know about such things may gain most useful information from this source. At head quarters, one of the Ambassadors has a document to present to the Sultan in person. The Ambassador has a cold. He is kept waiting in a wretched room, without a fire, for 2 hours. It is the duty of this high official to point out to His Majesty how dan-gerous is the course he is pursuing, and how it might imperil his throne. To which the Sultan replies that unless the Ambassador goes home soon, and is quickly

D

in bed, it will be dangerous for him.* The Sultan
scores again ; he always does, or has up to now.
How long, oh how long, *can* it last ? is the bitter cry
of millions. Most of the troops are unpaid, and are,
therefore, tempted to join in the massacres and
robberies they are sent to suppress. When will a
much needed Cromwell or Garibaldi arise ? And,
civilization echoes, when ?

* A story something like this was reported in one of the newspapers
as occuring to our English representative, and contradicted, but I stick
to my tale as it stands.

HERBERT JOINS THE AUSTRIAN LLOYD STEAMER.

CHAPTER IX.

D O my countrymen know what they are doing? If my readers will bear with me, I will at least try to inform them. Liberals, Radicals, Tories, or whatever you may be, you are, one and all, with the best intentions possible, doing the stupidest thing on earth. You hold meetings, you force the hands of the Government. That Government threatens, but it cannot carry out its threats. As I write, I realize how pleased the Sultan is at watching your impotence. You have taught him how to misgovern his country, even in a worse manner than before; for, until you induced him to send troops to put down the Armenian atrocities, he was not aware that his soldiers, by joining forces with the Kurds, and helping them to further massacre their neighbours, could pay themselves the arrears due to them. Then, by promoting their commanders, and distributing orders, he has shown the world how completely he approves of this method of military payment. If my countrymen would help the Armenians, they have two courses, and only two, open to them. One is to let bad alone, and not make it worse. The other is to give Russia a mission (if she will accept it), and let her over-run and police the country. She will never leave it, we all know that. This goes without saying. Of course, I am aware of the binding nature of the treaty of Berlin. Possibly, some day we in England may learn what Russia is always teaching us, viz., that circumstances alter cases, even in regard to the most sacred of treaties. Need I mention certain fortifications in the Black Sea, which have been erected in direct defiance of a very solemn engagement, but then in came the convenient circumstances, which a great power considered had altered her obligations. I hope my reader, who has bought a book on yachting, will forgive me this slight digression; he will, however, be the first to agree with me, that it is impossible to yacht with one's eyes shut.

We did not go further up the Bosphorus, for the weather was bad, and excursions inland, which would have been interesting, were too dangerous, the state of the country generally being far from settled. If the surrounding district should, in due course, become only slightly more civilized, tourists will find here beautiful scenery well worth a visit, and really good sport of all descriptions, particularly wild fowl shooting, which will well repay them. Just now this might become *too* exciting. If anyone should be tempted to try, then on no account go alone, or even with a party, unless accompanied by some person who, with a thorough knowledge of the country, knows how, when, and where to go. The Black Sea, or rather Sebastopol (its chief attraction), does not tempt us, as the difficulties now placed in the way of yachts entering the harbour are serious. Perhaps in a few

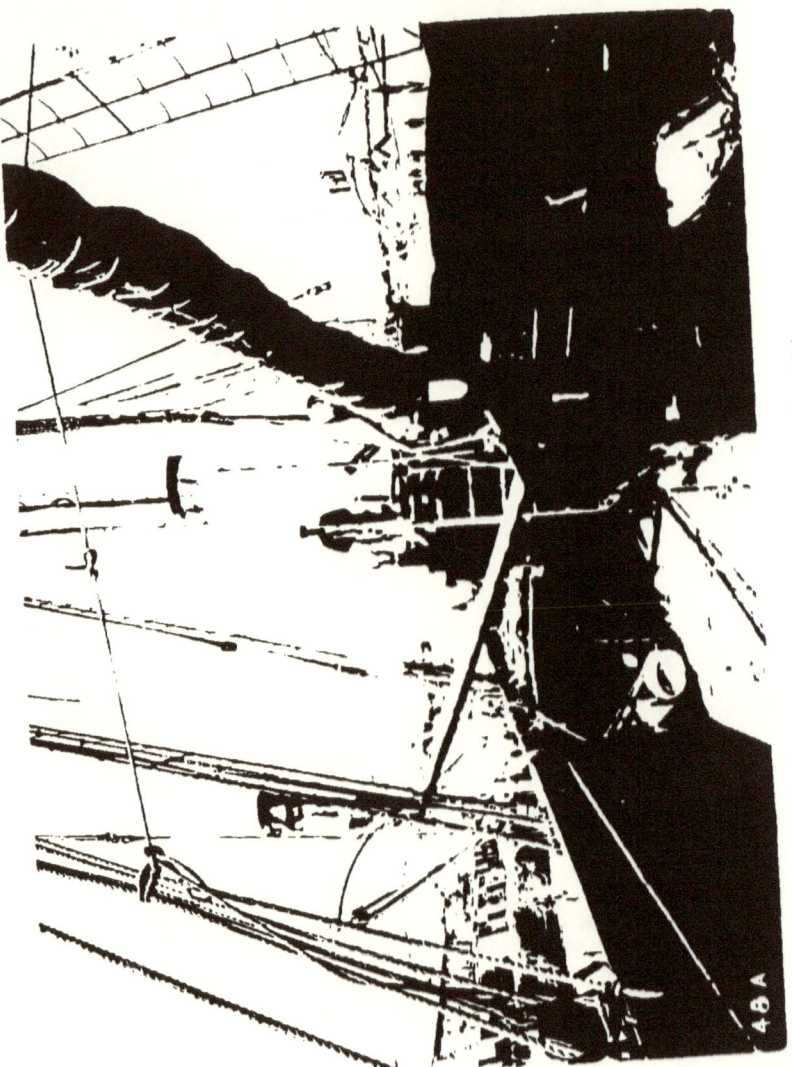

QUIET ANCHORAGE AFTER A GALE.

years, or even months, things may improve, but just now, if my friends will take my advice, they will make very special enquiries at the Embassy before entering on their expeditions.

Of the mouths of the Danube, I can only speak from hear-say evidence. I have spoken to the captains of several trading steamers, and received from them very little encouragement to go in that direction. If, however, a desire is felt to visit these parts, please remember that the ice is often dangerous to vessels late in February, or even in March. May or September are the best months to go there, and then (if you can) get an experienced pilot to take you. At the Consulate at Galata, you will find English friends who will give you the best advice on most points in connection with Black Sea pilots, Black Sea navigation, and the Black Sea trade, if you care to enquire. Circumstances may drive a man (as I was driven), to see Constantinople in mid-winter or not at all. Should my reader be as unfortunately placed as I was, then I would say to you let your first thought be given to your stoves; see that you have enough of them, and that they are the best money can buy. I have no object in recommending any stoves, and there may be better ones than the "Cera," sold by the Glasgow Cera Light Company. I, however, use these myself, and have for some years; if anyone knows of a better, I shall be glad of the information. Take out with you the very warmest rugs and coats, and wraps, that London can produce. Give your men an extra blanket apiece (this is *all* important). Mind that your anchors and cables are quite beyond criticism, and then harden your heart and keep your temper as long as you can. If you bring your vessel to an anchor at Stamboul, and leave that harbour again without loss of this commodity, then the Book of Job must henceforward be regarded as quite an insufficient study: to write a book will then become your duty, so as to inform the world how you did it. I watched several vessels entering and leaving, as well as the conduct of their several Captains, and the authorized Version, in regard to patience, still remains my model.

The passage home again through the Dardanelles suggests, only very naturally, a series of questions. Trained, as I happened to be, in Her Majesty's Navy, I naturally was taught to believe that *nothing* was, or could be, impossible for British sailors to accomplish. Perhaps, therefore, my remarks may require to be read with a margin. I distinctly remember, when hearing of the Charge of the Light Brigade at Balaclava (I actually did hear the guns), that could 600 blue jackets have ridden the charge, they would have done it better. This creed, as a bellicose one for Naval combatants generally, cannot be surpassed, so I decline now to state that the English fleet, or at least some of them, might not force the passage of the Dardanelles, even without aid from a land force; but this, perhaps, I may say, that all the other Navies in the world combined would find the evening after the action by far the pleasantest part of the day, that is if any of their crews lived to enjoy it.

That a combined land and sea force could capture
the Dardanelles I do not doubt, but the authority
which ordered an Admiral to pass the Dardanelles,
without a sufficient land force to help him, would
be culpable to the last degree. I do not think a
book, which any one might buy, the place in which
to put on record what I know of the strength of the
Dardanelles, or of the forces which are always available to resist attack. The yachtsman's position I
conceive should always be one void of offence. We
owe so much to all nations and all peoples, for their
kindness to us and our craft, that I think politics,
naval and military matters, and disputes generally,
are better left alone, unless the writer has a happy
knack of touching these questions with a very light
hand indeed. I confess that, as regards Turkey, I
have found my rule almost impossible to carry out,
certainly as conscientiously as I could have wished;
but if I have erred in this respect, I believe in what I
have written I have the sympathy of the whole
civilized world with me.

CHAPTER X.

 N January 12th, we sailed from Constantinople, and passed the night at Buzuk Chekmejeh, a very comfortable bay to anchor in; then to Kutali roads in the morning. Bad weather, of course.

January 14th, sailed early for Gallipoli, as we wanted to catch a steamer bound for Constantinople, Herbert having to return. We arrived in good time to do this, when the saddest of partings took place. We had enjoyed ourselves together so much that it was hard work saying good-bye.

January 15th, sailed from Gallipoli, and anchored in Niagara Liman. This is the bay in which all ships are bound to stop to get their pratique, and show the Sultan's firman authorizing them to pass through the Dardanelles.* After waiting an hour, we weighed again and proceeded to Morto Bay, near the entrance of the Dardanelles, and there anchored. I should like to have given photos of many points of interest between Gallipoli and the Western entrance, but the

---

* The extreme inconvenience of not being allowed to pass the Dardanelles at night is felt by all nations, and is complained of by all, but there seems now to be no hope that the old established rule will be relaxed, or even modified.

SAMSON'S STONE, ISLAND OF SAMOS.

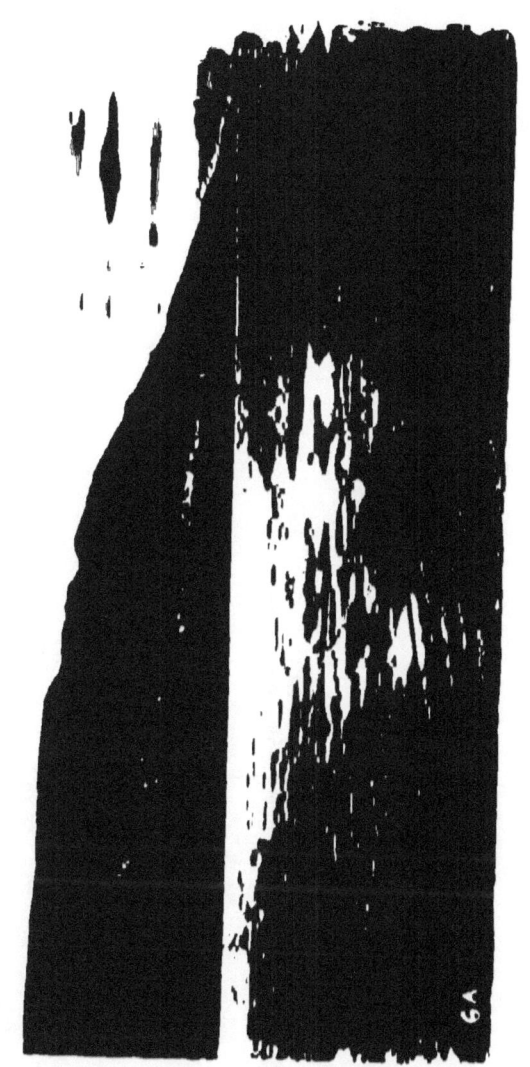

CAPE BABA, ASIA MINOR.

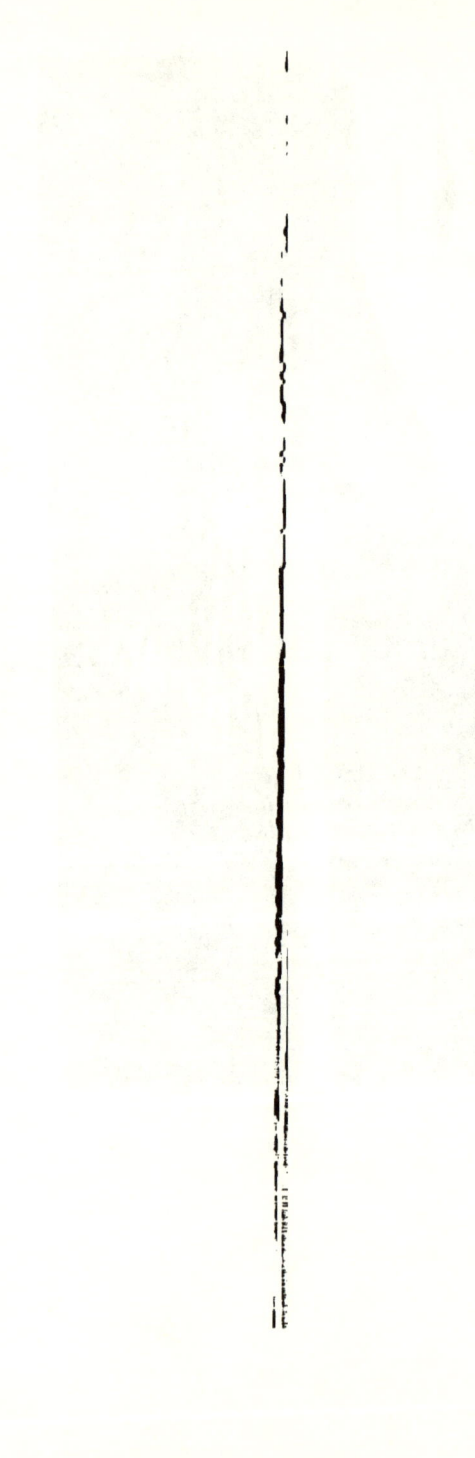

SCALA NUOVA.

whole of the narrows bristles with forts, and my readers will understand the dangers as well as the difficulties of so doing. Apart from the·forts, there is little to interest in the winter time, as the want of verdure makes the banks on each side look bare; they are white with snow, and wholly uninteresting. There is fair anchorage ground on each side of the entrance of the Dardanelles, but, if you have bad luck, it is sure to come on to blow from the quarter you are not protected from.

On the morning of January 16th, we weighed, and proceeded to Gymno Island, opposite to Mitylene. A splendid North-Easterly breeze sending us along 10 or 11 knots until we entered the Strait. Here, with a glass falling faster than I ever remember before, and the weather becoming both thick and rainy, I decided to get the nearest shelter I could, and found a very snug anchorage inside the Gymno Light, and close under the land in 8 fathoms. Yachtsmen come here and spend a quiet night, and do not be tempted to that worst of ports in Mitylene, where my pilot once persuaded me to anchor. I bought my experience at the cost of two restless nights in a gale of wind in the aforesaid open harbour.

There is one advantage in yachting in this part of the world in the winter,—one learns a good deal. I had now given my cousins, Major and Mrs. L., a good sample of sea-life. They thoroughly enjoyed it, proved good sailors, and worked like two slaves at their self-imposed photographic task. They have taken several pictures since they joined, and thoroughly entered into the spirit of the undertaking.

42

To be successful, one must work hard at this as at everything else.

January 17th. We had not intended going to sea on the next day, but a temporary lull in the morning tempted us out, and we ran before the gale to Foujes, or Foggia, harbour, having got a good photo of Gymno harbour and lighthouse on our way out. What a comfortable little harbour this is, and how doubly welcome when one has been roughly handled and tossed about in a gale. The harbour-master is civility itself, and, while you are getting pratique, offers you the best coffee possible. I bought about 40 old coins here for a small sum, in the hope that some of them might prove genuine and valuable. They will have to pass under the critical eye of an expert when we reach the Piræus. The demand for old coins is so common, that it is really impossible to satisfy travellers, without adding a large per-centage of spurious ones. So says my guide, and he is a man of experience. My only hope lies in the fact that this is an out-of-the-way place, and that the ordinary tourist comes here but seldom. I have previously mentioned the industry of the Greek inhabitants of these seaport towns, but what I think would strike a new comer most, is the fact that so much splendid land is left to waste. A few olive trees are planted here and there, but, as a rule, on these islands and along the coast, one sees thousands of acres which would yield splendid produce if well cultivated. The curse of Turkish rule and Turkish mismanagement is over the land, and what might be a prosperous country remains a standing reproach to civilization.

FOREIGN CRUISERS IN TURKISH WATERS.

43

January 18th. To Smyrna : blowing again, of course, but picked out a good anchorage inshore, opposite the Sporting Club. So heavy were the squalls during the night that I let go a second anchor. Two Italian, two Russian, and two French men-of-war were anchored here. The British Consul-General, who I called upon, had his hands full. Reports from various quarters showed that there was a very uneasy feeling abroad, and troops had to be dispatched to places along the coast to keep order. In Smyrna itself there is not much danger, as the majority of the inhabitants are Christian, and Mohammedan fanaticism would fail in its object, if anything like a massacre were attempted. There being ships of war at anchor here belonging to European nations, we feel quite secure. The late Grand Vizier, Kiamil Pasha, is the Governor-General, and as he is, unquestionably, one of the most able, as he certainly is one of the most enlightened of his class, no danger is anticipated. The Ramazan begins in about three weeks. This is likely to be a very trying time in outlying districts. In most of the Turkish Islands, the Greek population outnumbers the Tufkish, so nothing will happen there. It is more in Asia Minor proper where there is cause for alarm. I cannot give a better description of the stagnation in trade, which, in consequence of this uneasy feeling, affects all classes, than by stating, that of the Austrian Lloyd steamers which I saw trading to Constantinople, not one of them carried the full cargo allowed them as mail steamers ; while on board the one which Herbert joined to take him from Gallipoli to Constantinople, he was absolutely the only 1st class passenger on board. She ought to have carried 60, at least.

January 19th. Still blowing hard. It being Sunday, the crews of the foreign men-of-war have leave on shore, and the amount of drunken men, and rows in the streets, could not have been surpassed by Portsmouth itself in the good old days, when it seemed to be Jack's first duty to let the inhabitants realize that he was on shore.

January 20th. Coaled and watered. There is no place that I have yet visited where coaling and watering requires more attention. The prices must be fixed beforehand, of course. Then, if after all you get your full weight of coal or full quantity of water, you will be lucky. The Consul-General can give some good advice about this. The one thing to avoid, is to enter into an arrangement with any of the rascals who come on board to tout for custom here. The washing you send ashore, if through a broker, is 3s. 6d. a dozen ; if sent to a man whose name I have left at the Consul General's office, it is 2s. 6d. a dozen. The same man undertakes the washing in both cases.

Thursday, 21st, I called on His Highness Kiamil Pasher (late Grand Vizier). He is a very interesting man. He was most kind and communicative, and speaks the most fluent English. On January 22nd, the next day, he returned the call at the Consul General's house. His view of the Armenian difficulty I am not at liberty to publish, but I may say that it differs *toto cœlo* from that which is commonly held by the majority of Europeans. Circumstances which have

since transpired have convinced me that His Highness
was not far wrong. As Grand Vizier at the time of
the Egyptian Convention negotiated by Sir Drum-
mond Wolff on the part of England, he had, of
course, a very leading part to play. When accurately
informed, and he is very well informed, I could
imagine, were he given full powers, that he would
act in a manner which few statesmen could find
much fault with; but accurate information is very
difficult to obtain,—it is almost impossible. Poor
Turkey! poor Turkey! when will your day of
enlightenment arrive?

Chapter XI.

ANUARY 23rd, we sailed for our old and favourite anchorage of Foujes before described, and, having passed a quiet night there, left next morning, January 24th, for Sigajik Harbour, a very snug and comfortable anchorage. Yachtsmen, if you are cruising in this part of the world, and if you want a perfect anchorage and a quiet night, do no forget this port; good milk and fresh eggs await you in the morning. This harbour is difficult to find by day, but it is worth hunting for; I should say at night it is out of the question, there being no lights to guide you.

Next day, January 25th, to Scala Nova, 6 miles from Ephesus. Of the temple of Diana there remains hardly a ruin, but the port from which most of her devotees disembarked to do her honour remains still in a flourishing condition. Mr. W. (a gentleman owning a mine in the district) joined us here, and we take him for a shooting expedition. The anchorage is exposed from West to North, so we quit the interesting scene for a more sheltered harbour. This we found in the evening at Tigani, a port on the East of Samos Island. There is 4 fathoms inside the breakwater, and from 6 to 8

LIGHTHOUSE, TIGANE, ISLAND OF SAMOS.

SIQHAJIK HARBOUR.

SIQHAJIK ENTRANCE.

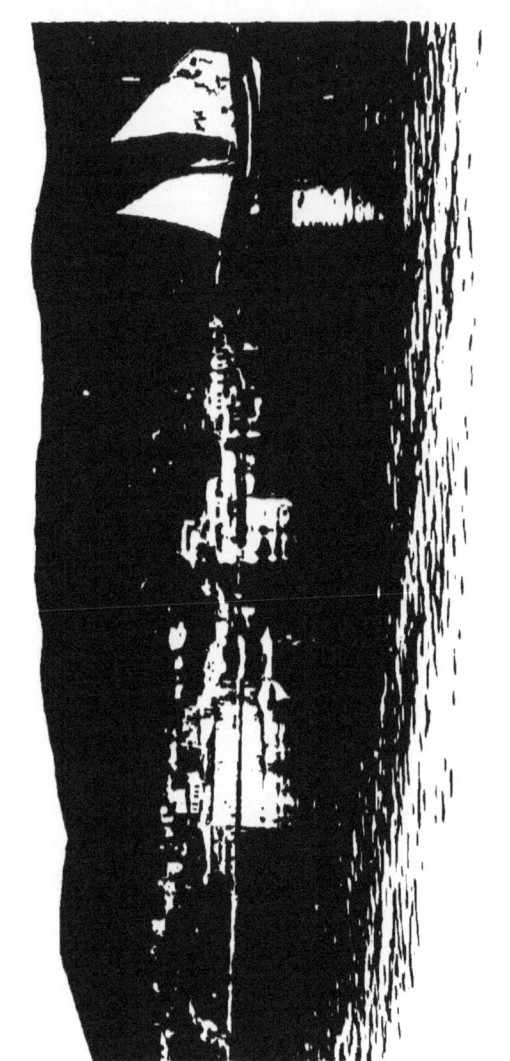

SHOOTING QUARTERS, CHI LUKOI, ASIA MINOR.

fathoms outside. We anchored in 7 fathoms and in perfect shelter from the North wind which was then blowing.

January 26th, we left our anchorage in a gale, but it kept on moderating all day, and when we entered the snug little harbour of Chelukoi in Mundayah Bay we found a calm. I took a walk on shore to the top of the hill, to inspect our shooting ground for the morrow. What a view opened out. Some thousands of wild duck and geese were to be seen swimming about in the streams, which intersected a marsh 5 miles across and 8 miles long. This marsh has been celebrated for its wild boar and game for many a long year. To-morrow we are to go and prove its worth.

To-morrow comes, and the beaters are *not* ready; it takes a long time to get beaters ready in the East. We go the next day, however, and get really fine sport, 9 wild boar killed and 3 wounded. The last named will all be gathered, as the vultures will show where they can be found. We stay on for a few days after this enjoying the wild fowl shooting, and, on February 1st, bid adieu to our friends and sail for Patmos. I must not omit to state that our host, on whose estate we were shooting, was Mehmet Bey, a real Turk, and a real sportsman, to my mind, quite a remarkable combination. We suffered, here, from too much attention throughout our visit, as the Governor of the place insisted on an escort of 3 foot soldiers and 2 mounted guards. Rather in the way, all of them. Mr. W., who was most kind, translated for us. He is the Manager of an English Company, who are engaged in exploring for mines in Asia Minor, and forming Companies to work them. The work is arduous, and he and his friends will certainly deserve any profits which may be derived from their labours. I am glad to say they have begun well, but the security which good government gives to trade and security of tenure are not certainties here. The Company has, however, in spite of all drawbacks, managed to open out a not inconsiderable trade, and the authorities seem fairly sanguine as to the future. Capitalists, both at Smyrna and elsewhere, have much money invested here, and, if things settle down, they ought to reap a good harvest. They certainly well deserve it. Persons interested in mining might do worse than make enquiries in this direction.

Port Stavros, in the Island of Patmos, was reached at 3 in the afternoon, and I landed to converse with any natives I came across. An old Greek priest and his female cousin welcomed my pilot (who was translating for me) and myself. They treated us most kindly, offering every hospitality. Our host was one of 50 priests who either live in the large monastery on the hill top, or are quartered in little cottages near the small chapels which are dotted about the island. He told me that their tradition was that St. John the Evangelist wrote the gospel that goes by his name, and the Apocalypse, in a small cottage where the monastery now stands, and that the vision vouchsafed to him was delivered while he was laying with his head on a stone (which is shown), half way down the hill on the Eastern

VIEW FROM ANCHORAGE, GYMNOS.

side of the island. A small but very picturesque
little church is built over this stone. I was much
astonished at finding a peasant on the island (a
magnificent looking man) who had never even heard
of St. John; he informed me that if I wanted
information about the Apostle, as he was a saint,
doubtless one of the priests could inform me, as it
was their business. Port Stavros is not an advisable
harbour, nor one I could recommend, except to
spend a few hours at, and then only in fine weather.
Port Scala, on the Eastern side, is much better in
every way. I only anchored at the former port
because it was handy to leave from in the early
morning, as I wanted, if possible, to reach Syra
harbour (80 miles off) next day. It may interest
my reader to hear, that before bidding my final adieu
to the friendly priest who welcomed me, he showed
me his gun, and asked if I could possibly spare
him some gunpowder, as there many woodcock on the
island, and he was fond of shooting. A priest's life
here seems not altogether an unpleasant one. He
offered me the best coffee I have yet tasted, and a
capital cigarette to smoke, while from an ample flask
he produced some wine which he had made himself,
and he was very proud of. A very choice grape is
grown on the Southern slopes of the island.

The Archimandrite lives in the monastery. He
speaks a little English, having been at the head of the
Greek Community in New York a few years back.
I can imagine no greater contrast than life in Patmos
and in New York. There is a library attached to
the monastery, containing many interesting works.

E

50

The Greek Archbishop at Athens can supply information of what it contains, should any visitors to the Piræus feel interested. I tried to leave Patmos two days after my arrival, but had to put back, a strong North East gale, which I could not run before, was blowing, and a very heavy sea was running.

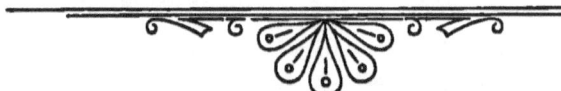

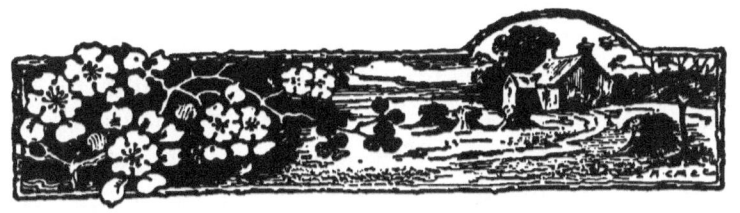

CHAPTER XII.

OT till February 4th did I venture out, and then had first to keep under shelter of Nikaria Island, and then run before a whole gale to our old anchorage at Delos. There was a terrific sea running, and I was very grateful when we arrived, and could let go both anchors under the shelter of old Lazaretto point. The wind was still blowing a gale. Does it ever leave off in these parts? Some Greek sailors, belonging to a small schooner we found at anchor here, told us they had been wind-bound for a month, and a gale had been blowing all the time. I quite believed them, for we had hardly experienced one fine day during our visit to Asia Minor, or, indeed, for a very long time.

Next day, February 5th, we sailed for Syra, a charming harbour, clean town, good coal (cheap) 19s. a ton, best Cardiff coal too, good spring water also, 3s. a ton. Civility is the order of the day, and yachtsmen must be hard, indeed, to please if they are not satisfied here. There is an Italian Opera House, and, during the season, a good company is generally engaged in producing the most popular operas of the

day, and in very creditable style. We came in for
the Prima Donna's benefit, and were pleased with all
we saw and heard. The Mayor of the town had
most kindly placed his box at our disposal. At
almost all the ports at which we have called, and
above all at Syra, I have been very painfully op-
pressed by the thought of how impossible it was to
return, in any way, the many little acts of kindness
and civility, which have been so liberally showered
upon us.

February 7th, we sailed for the Piræus, and arrived
on the 8th, having spent the night at the St. Nikolo
anchorage, in the Island of the Zea. Oddly enough,
fine weather the whole way. Before quitting this
interesting locality, an account of the Maid of
Athens and her family, from the travels of the late
artist, Mr. H. Williams, who lodged, as Lord Byron
did, in the house of Theodore Macri, may interest :—

"Our servant, who had gone before to procure accommodation, met us at the gate, and conducted us to
Theodore Macri, the Consulina's, where we at present
live. This lady is the widow of the Consul, and has
three lovely daughters ; the eldest celebrated for her
beauty, and said to be the 'Maid of Athens' of Lord
Byron. Their apartment is immediately opposite to
ours, and if you could see them as we do now, through
the gently waving aromatic plants before our window,
you would leave your heart in Athens. Theresa (the
'Maid of Athens'), Catinca, and Mariana are of middle
stature. On the crown of the head of each is a red
Albanian skull-cap, with a blue tassel spread out and
fastened down like a star. Near the edge or bottom of
the skull-cap, is a handkerchief of various colours bound

LIGHTHOUSE, PORT ST. NIKOLO, ISLAND OF ZEA.

round their temples. The youngest wears her hair loose, falling on her shoulders, the hair behind descending down the back nearly to the waist, and, as usual, tied with silk. The two eldest generally have their hair bound, and fastened under the handkerchief. Their upper robe is a pelisse edged with fur, hanging loose down to the ankles; below is a handkerchief of muslin covering the bosom, and terminating at the waist, which is short; under that a gown of striped silk or muslin, with a gore round the swell of the loins, falling in front in graceful negligence; white stockings and yellow slippers complete their attire. The two eldest have black, or dark hair and eyes; their visage oval, and complexion somewhat pale, with teeth of dazzling whiteness. Their cheeks are rounded, and noses straight, rather inclined to aquiline. The youngest, Mariana, is very fair, her face not so finely rounded, but has a gayer expression than her sisters, whose countenances, except when the conversation has something of mirth in it, may be said to be rather pensive. Their persons are elegant, and their manners pleasing and ladylike, such as would be fascinating in any country. They possess very considerable powers of conversation, and their minds seems to be more instructed than those of the Greek women in general. With such attractions, it would indeed be remarkable if they did not meet with great attentions from the travellers who occasionally are resident in Athens. They sit in the Eastern style, a little reclined, with their limbs gathered under them on the divan, and without shoes. Their employments are the needle, tambouring, and reading."

But the beauty of the inhabitants, which has changed little since Mr. Williams' day, must not detain us, so I will only add that we have run into capital weather, both for photographing and enjoyment, so critics, I hope, will not complain of any want of pictures round about the Piræus, taken in this cruise, which I have added to some given in my last work.*

On February 10th, we sailed for the entrance of the Gulf of Corinth, and spent the night in the bay anchorage just outside of its Eastern entrance, and, of course, also of the canal. Some repairs to our machinery were done during the night, at the workshop the Company have built here ; they also supplied us with water, both very cheap and good. On the 11th, we passed the canal, and anchored in the Gulf of Vostitza. A lovely night followed, quite worth recording, so calm and still. Bread, meat, and milk can be got here, and the best water in Greece. Yachtsmen please note this, it may be of use to you. Anchor off the inner lighthouse, please, in 9 fathoms, or even in 8, and you will be within 200 yards of the water I speak of. In the morning lovely weather again, and we are off to Ithaca. The morning after that, to Corfu, and, after two days, across to Gallipoli in Italy. I do not say anything about Ithaca where, of course, we called, but Corfu is such a centre for all yachtsmen that I cannot help quoting Murray in *extenso*, not only because I know of no better or shorter historical sketch of the Island, up to the date when the English turned the Ionian Islands over to Greece ; but I venture to hope that when the traveller or yachtsman has seen my photos and read this extract, as well as my own remarks in both my

---

* " With the Yacht, Camera, and Cycle in the Mediterranean."

books, he will have in his mind as clear an idea of the Island as he can hope for:—

"INNS AND ACCOMMODATION FOR TRAVELLERS, &c.

The best hotels at Corfu are The Hotel de St. George, The Club Hotel, The Hotel · d'Europe, The Hotel d'Orient, and La Bella Venezia. Here, as in the South of Europe generally, a bargain should be made for meals and accommodation. Saddle horses may be hired at Corfu for about a dollar a day; if taken for a week or a month, the charge diminishes in proportion. Carriages may likewise be engaged in the same manner.

There is a small inn at Argostoli, the chief town of Cephalonia; and another in Zante, the accommodation in which is very bad. There are no inns in the smaller islands, though lodgings may be procured in all of them.

There are Theatres at Corfu and Cephalonia, where Italian Operas are given during the winter, and plays and amateur representations at other seasons.

British subjects will have no trouble about their luggage or passport landing in the Ionian Islands.*

1. Corfu.

It may safely be asserted, without prejudice to the poetical fame of Ithaca, that of all the Ionian Islands, Corfu is the one in which, in all ages, the most important part on the stage of history has been played. From the peculiar character of its beautiful scenery and delightful climate, it forms a connecting link between the East and the West, like Madeira between the old world and the new. Its geographical position on the high road of

---

* They have very little now. C.

navigation between Greece and Italy, has made Corfu a possession of great importance both in ancient and in modern times. 'Here (Thucydides, vi. 42) was passed in review that splendid armament which was destined to perish at Syracuse, the Moscow of Athenian ambition. Here, 400 years later, the waters of Actium saw a world lost and won. Here again, after the lapse of sixteen centuries, met together those Christian powers which, off Lepanto, dealt to the Turkish fleet, so long the scourge and terror of Europe, a blow from which it has never recovered.' But our space will allow us to draw only an outline of the glories of Corfu, the seat of government in these regions under both the Venetians and the English, and for so many ages the key of the Adriatic, and one of the main outposts of Christendom.

The ancients universally regarded Corcyra as identical with the Homeric Scheria (derived, perhaps, from the Phœnician Schara commerce) where the enterprising and sea-loving Phæacians dwelt, governed by their King Alcinous. The island is said also to have been called from its shape, Drepane, or the Sickle; it describes a curve, the convexity of which is towards the W.; its length from N.W. to S.E. is about 40 miles; the breadth is greatest in the N., where it is nearly 20 miles, but it gradually tapers towards its S. extremity. The historical name of Corcyra appears first in 'Herodotus.' About B.C. 734, a colony was planted here by the Corinthians; and that maritime activity, for which the Corcyræans were afterwards celebrated, may have partly arisen from the fusion of the Dorians with the original inhabitants. Homer states that the Phæacians had come from Sicily; but it seems probable that they were a branch of the Liburnians, that enterprising and seafaring people, who long continued to occupy the more Northernly islands in the Adriatic along the Dalmatian and Illyrian shores. Corcyra soon became rich and powerful by its extensive commerce, and founded many colonies on the neighbouring mainland, such as Epidamnus, Apollonia, Leucas, and Anactorium. So rapid was their prosperity, that the colonists soon became formidable rivals of their mother country, and, about B.C. 665, a battle was fought between their fleets, which is memorable as the most ancient seafight on record. Corcyra appears to have been subjugated by Periander (Herod iii., 49, seq.) but to have recovered its independence. During the Persian war the Corcyræans are stated by Herodotus (vii., 168) to have played false to the national cause, and their names did not appear on the muster-roll of Salamis. At a later period, Corcyra, by invoking the aid of Athens against the Corinthians, became one of the proximate causes of the Peloponesian war. During the progress of that contest, her political power and importance were irretrievably ruined, in consequence of the fierce factions and civil dissensions which agitated the island, and in which both the aristocratical and popular parties were guilty of the most horrible atrocities. It has been truly observed, that 'it was the state of parties and of politics at Corcyra, that the greatest of ancient historians made the subject of a solemn disquisition, considering that they were a type of the general condition of Greece at the period of the Peloponesian war, and that the picture which he then drew of his countrymen belongs, in its main outlines, to all ages and nations. He who would discuss that most interesting problem, the state and prospects of the Modern Greeks, can hardly do wrong in adopting for his observations the same basis as Thucydides.'

For some generations after the Peloponesian war, the fortunes of Corcyra were various. Though it appears never to have recovered its former political consequence, a gorgeous picture of the fertility and opulence of the island, in B.C. 373, has been drawn by Xenophon (Hellen, vi. 2). When it was invaded in that year by the Spartans, under Mnasippus, it is represented as being in the highest state of cultivation and full of the richest produce; with fields admirably tilled, and vineyards in surpassing condition; with splendid farm-buildings, well appointed wine-cellars, and abundance of cattle. The hostile soldiers, we are told, while enriching themselves by their depredations, became so pampered by the plenty around them, that they refused to drink any wine that was not of the first quality. At a later period, the island was alternately seized by the Spartans, the Athenians, and the Macedonians. King Pyrrhus, of Epirus, occupied it during his Italian wars; and it finally fell under the Roman dominion B.C. 229. From its situation near Brundisium and Dyrrachium, the Dover and Calais of the ancients, Corcyra was frequently visited by illustrious Romans. Here Augustus assembled his fleet before the battle of Actium, and we have notices of the presence of Tibullus, Cato, and of Cicero, whose friend, Atticus, possessed large estates on the opposite coast of Epirus, probably in the plain of Butrinto, now so much resorted to by English shooting parties. The last mention of Corcyra in the ancient authors seems to have been that by Suetonius, who relates that the Emperor Nero, on his way to Greece, sang and danced before the altar of Jupiter at Cassiope.

Henceforward, there is little notice of Corfu until the times of the Crusades, when its geographical position caused it to be greatly frequented. Robert Guiscard seized the island in A.D. 1081, during his wars with the Eastern Empire; and another great Norman chief, Richard I., of England, landed here on his return from the Holy Land in A.D. 1193. After remaining in the island for some time, he continued his voyage to Ragusa, whence, proceeding by land towards his dominions, he was made captive by the Duke of Austria.

During the decline of the Empire, Corfu underwent many changes of fortune, being sometimes in the hands of the Greek Emperors, sometimes in those of various Latin princes, particularly of the House of Anjou, then governing Naples, and always exposed to the incursions of freebooters and pirates. At length, A.D. 1389, the inhabitants sent a deputation to Venice, to implore the protection of that Republic, under whose sovereignty they remained until its downfall in A.D. 1797. We have already drawn an outline of the political condition of the Ionians under Venetian rule, and of their subsequent fortunes until united to the kingdom of Greece. Venice made Corfu her principal arsenal and *point d'appui* in Greece, and surrounded the town with extensive and massive fortifications, which set at defiance the whole power of the Ottomans, in the assaults of 1537 and 1570, and, above all, in the celebrated siege of 1716, remarkable as the last great attempt of the Turks to extend their conquests in Christendom. On this occasion, the Republic was fortunate in its selection as Commandment at Corfu of Marshal Schulemberg, a brave and skilful German soldier of fortune, who had served under Prince Eugene, and the King of Saxony. While directing the retreat of a division of the Saxon army before the Swedes, he had formerly extricated himself, when apparently lost, by throwing his forces over the river Oder, a manœuvre which drew from

60

Charles XII. himself the exclamation, 'Schulemberg has conquered us to-day!' A statue of the Marshal, erected by the Senate of Venice, stands on the esplanade at Corfu, in front of the gate of the citadel.*

The Turkish fleet of 60 ships of war, and a number of smaller vessels, appeared before the place on July 5th, 1716; they were commanded by the Capitan-Pasha or Lord High Admiral of the Empire in person; while the Seraskier or General-in-Chief led the army of 30,000 picked troops, which was ferried across by the boats of the fleet from Butrinto to Govino. On July 8th, the Venetian fleet entered the northern channel, and, by saluting the Virgin of Cassopo, gave notice of their approach to the Turks, who might otherwise have been taken at a disadvantage. During the subsequent siege, neither party felt sufficiently strong to force on a sea-fight, but stood, as it were, at bay, the Ottoman vessels stretching across from Butrinto to Govino, and the Venetians from Vido to Sayada.

On July 16th, the Seraskier established his head-quarters at Potamo, and laid waste the country far and wide, the peasantry having mostly taken refuge within the walls of the town. The garrison amounted to 5,000 men, chiefly Germans, Slavonians, and Italians. The Turks erected batteries on Mount Olivetto, above the suburb of Manduchio, on August 1st, and, after several failures, carried Mount Abraham by assault, on August 3rd. Their advanced works were then abandoned by the besieged, when the Turks pushed their approaches through the suburb of Castrades, and closely invested the town. For several days, there were frequent assaults by the Infidels and sorties of the Christians, with heavy

---

* A sister of Schulemberg was one of the two mistresses of George I. of Great Britain, and was by him created Duchess of Kendal.

ALBANIAN BOYS.

losses on both sides, the inhabitants, including, it is said, even the priests and the women, fighting along with the soldiers on the ramparts and in the trenches. An hour before daybreak, on August 19th, the Turks made their grand assault, and effected a lodgment in Scarponi, an outwork of Port Neuf. Schulemberg then headed a sally in person, and, after a desparate contest, drove them from this vantage-ground with immense loss. In the night of the 22nd, they retreated to Govino, re-embarked, and sailed away to Constantinople, where both the Admiral and General paid with their lives the penalty of their failure. The Turks abandoned in their trenches all their ammunition and stores, including 78 pieces of artillery; and they are stated to have lost, during the siege of five weeks, full half their army in action and by disease, for it was the most deadly period of a very unhealthy season. The Venetians lost 2,000 out of their garrison of 5,000 men.*

The first approach to Corfu, whether from the North or the South, is extremely striking. The South Channel will be described hereafter (section ii., Rte. 1). Coming from the North, the traveller sails close under those

> 'Thunder cliffs of fear,
> The Acroceraunian mountains of old fame.'

An uninterrupted lofty chain, rising abruptly from the

---

* An excellent account of the seige of Corfu in 1716, will be found in the 'Corps Papers of the Royal Engineers,' Vol. 1. pp. 262—272.

The best special authorities on the antiquities and history of the island, are:—

'Historia di Corfu,' da Andrea Marmora, Venice, 1672 ; which contains much curious information, and several prints of the town and fortresses in their mediæval aspect.

'Primordia Corcyra,' cura A. M. Quirini, 1725 ; a treatise in Latin on the antiquities of Corfu, by a Roman Catholic Archbishop of the Island.

'Illustrazioni Corciresi,' da Andrea Mustoxidi, Milano, 1811 ; comments on the history of his native island by a Corfoit noble of literary distinction.

'Le tre Constituzioni delle Isole,' Corfu, 1850 ; a valuable collection of official documents, &c., throwing light on the more recent history of the Ionian Islands.

very brink of the sea in precipitous cliffs or rugged declivities, and terminating in craggy peaks, capped with snow during nine months of the year. Here and there an Albanian hamlet hangs like a snow wreath on the mountain-side. Wherever there is a break in the heavy masses of cloud, which robe so often the further summits of the Pindus range, and the sun of Greece tints them at mid-day with golden, at even with rosy radiance, the mind delights to figure to itself, far away amid those dim mysterious crags, the region of the 'wintry Dodona,' now shorn indeed of its ancient sanctity and honour, but still tenanted, as in Homer's time, by a race 'with unwashed feet and sleeping on the ground.' (Il. xvi., 235).

As we advance, the coast of Corfu rises to the South-ward, presenting a long swelling mountain ridge,

'Spread like a shield upon the dark blue sea.'—Od. v., 281.

The outlines of the harbour are very graceful; and its surface is a dark mass of luxuriant groves of olives, cypress, and ilex. The Eastern extremity of the mountain ridge of San Salvador (the Istone of the ancients) projects within 2 miles of the mainland. On the right, the vessel passes the ruined walls of the mediæval fortress of Cassopo, erected on the site of the Hellenic city of Cassiope; on the left opens the plains or valley of Butrinto, the ancient Buthrontum, where Æneas was entertained by his kinsman Helenus. On clearing this strait, the sea again expands into an open gulf between the two coasts, and the citadel and town of Corfu appear in sight, forming the centre of an amphitheatre of rich and varied scenery. In front, the green slopes of the islet of Vido form a breakwater for the harbour. The promontory on which the town is built terminates to the Eastward in the citadel, built on a huge isolated rock, with its summit split into two lofty peaks, the 'aeriæ Phæacum arces' of Virgil (Æn. iii., 291), from which the modern name of the island is derived. The hoary cliff is bound round with forts and batteries, while its base is strewn with white houses and barracks, perched like sea-fowl, wherever they can find a resting place. The ramparts and bastions mingle with Nature's own craggy fortifications, mantled by a profusion of cactuses, evergreens, and wild flowers.

Across the bay, the Albanian coast presents now a less rugged aspect. The ridges of snowy mountains retire further into the distance, while the hills in the immediate vicinity of the sea offer, by their bleak but varied landscape, a fine contrast to the richly wooded and cultivated shores of the island. In the general view of the town, the Palace, formerly of the Lord High Commissioner, and now of the King, stands out among the other buildings as prominently as did that of King Alcinous of old. (Od. vi., 300).

The channel, which separates Corfu from Albania, varies in breadth from 2 to 12 miles, and appears one noble lake from the harbour, whence its outlets are not visible. It certainly affords one of the most beautiful and stirring spectacles in the world. Its Northern extremity narrows until it is lost among lofty mountains, swelling each over each like the waves of the ocean; while, gradually widening as it extends to the Southward, it spreads round the indentations and promontories of the fair and fertile island. But the whole forms a scene which addresses itself to the eye and to the heart, rather than to the ear. The memory of those who have once beheld it will long carry a vivid impression, which they will find hard to describe in adequate language.

The ordinary landing-place is at the Health Office

mole, but there is another for men-of-war and yacht boats in the ditch of the citadel, whence a flight of steps lead immediately to the esplanade.

The esplanade occupies the space between the town and the citadel, and is laid out with walks and avenues of trees. On its Northern verge stands the Palace of white Maltese stone, ornamented with a colonnade in front, and flanked by the two gates of St. Michael and St. George, each of which frames a lovely picture of the sea and mountains. The Palace was erected under the administration of Sir Thomas Maitland, and contains a suite of excellent ball-rooms. The Casino, or villa of the King, was built by Sir Frederick Adam in a beautiful situation about a mile to the South of the town. At the Southern extremity of the esplanade is a terrace over-hanging the sea, a little circular temple erected in memory of Sir Thomas Maitland, and an obelisk in honour of Sir Howard Douglas. There is also a statue of Sir Frederick Adam in front of the Palace, and one of Marshal Schulemberg in front of the drawbridge which leads into the citadel. To the West, the side of the esplanade next the town is bounded by a lofty row of private houses, with an arched walk beneath them.

The stranger in Corfu had better devote his first hour of leisure to inspecting the splendid panoramic view of the town and island, presented from the summit of the citadel. The Greek garrison church is a large building with a Doric portico, at the South side of the citadel. The ramparts are of various ages; some of them dating as far back as A.D. 1550. At the opposite, or Western, extremity of the town, rises another fortress, erected by the Venetians at the end of the XVI. century, and still generally known as Fort Neuf, or La Fortezza Nuova. The hill on which it is built is less lofty and precipitous

ALBANIAN SHEPHERDS.

than that of the citadel. The fire of these two fortresses protects the harbour.*

The town, including its suburbs of Manduchio to the West and Castrades to the South, contains 24,091 inhabitants. There are 4,000 Latins, with an archbishop of their own, and 5,000 Jews, which latter live in a separate quarter of the town; the remainder of the people belong to the Greek Church.

The Cathedral, dedicated to Our Lady of the Cave, is situated on the Line Wall, not far from Fort Neuf. The oldest church in the island is in the suburb of Castrades, near the Strada Marina. It is dedicated to St. Janson and St. Sosipater, comrades of St. Paul, and who are related by tradition to have been the first preachers of Christianity in Corcyra. Though neglected, and re-paired in bad taste, this church is a very graceful specimen of Byzantine architecture, and seems to have been finally erected out of the materials of heathen temples. Several columns and other ancient fragments are also built into the walls of the church at Paleopolis, on the road to the One-gun Battery. There are a great many other churches, the most remarkable being that of St. Spiridion, the Patron Saint of Corfu, whose body is preserved in a richly ornamented case. The annual offerings at this shrine amount to a considerable sum, and are the property of a noble Corfiot family, to whom the church belongs. Three times a year the body of the Saint is carried in solemn procession around the esplanade, followed by the Greek clergy and all the native authorities. The sick are sometimes brought out and laid where the Saint may be carried over them. St. Spiridion was bishop of a see in Cyprus, and was one

---

* Or rather *did* so until recently ; now, improved naval ordinance has rendered doubtful the security of this position.—EDITOR.

F

of the Fathers of the Council of Nice in A.D. 325. After his death, his embalmed body was believed to have wrought many miracles. Various and contradictory accounts have been given of the cause and manner of its conveyance to Corfu.

The town underwent great improvements during the period of the British protectorate, but it is still cramped and confined. The main streets have been widened, sanitary regulations have been enforced, markets have been built, an efficient police organized here (as throughout the islands), new roads and approaches have been constructed, especially the Strada Marina round the Bay of Castrades, which now forms one of the most charming public promenades in Europe. Above all, a copious supply of water, of which the town was formerly destitute, has been brought in pipes from a source above Benizze,—a distance of 7 miles. The suburbs were formerly richly planted with olive and mulberry trees, but these were cut down by the French, in order to clear a space before the fortifications, and their removal is supposed to have contributed in some degree to the improved salubrity; fevers, however, are still prevalent in autumn, though they are rarely of a malignant character.

The late Bishop of Lincoln has remarked that Corfu is a sort of geographical mosaic, to which many countries of Europe have contributed colours. The streets are Italian in their style and name; the arcades, by which some of them are flanked, might have come from Padua or Bologna; the winged Lion of St. Mark is seen marching in stone along the old Venetian bastions: a stranger will hear Italian from the native gentry, Greek from the peasants, Arabic from the Maltese grooms and gardeners, Albanian from the white-kilted mountaineers

CORFU HARBOUR ENTRANCE.

of the opposite coast. He may see Ionian venders haggling for how much they are to receive for their wares in Greek obols, bearing the Venetian lion on one side and Britannia with her ægis on the other : no bad epitome of the modern history of the island, and forming a curious addition to the silver records which tell what Corfu was in past ages. The prow of a ship, a Triton striking with his trident, a galley in full sail, the gardens of Alcinous, and a Bacchus crowned with ivy—these are some of the monetary memorials of the ancient power, commerce, and fertility of Corcyra.

We have the authority of Thucydides for the identity of Corcyra with the Scheria or Phæacia of Homer ; but it is impossible to draw a map of the Homeric island which shall coincide with the existing localities. Ulysses was brought to the island by a North wind, which would seem to mark Fano as Calypso's isle. The only stream of any consequence is that which empties itself into the sea between Manduchio and Govino, while the tradition of the peasantry points to the Fountain of Cressida, a copious spring gushing out near the sea, 4 miles S.W. of the modern town, as the spot where the nymph-like Nausicæ and her train of maidens received the suppliant Ulysses. She is, perhaps, the most interesting character in all ancient poetry ; and we gladly turn from the savage feuds and massacres of the Peloponnesian war to the contemplation of the fair daughter of Alcinous.

But, wherever may have been the Phæacia of Homer, there can be no doubt but that the Corcyra of Thucydides occupied the peninsula between the channel and the Lagoon, now called Lake Calichiopulo, after a noble family of Corfu ; the shores of which were converted by the English into a race-course. Excavations in this direction everywhere produce sculptures, tombs (such as

F 2

that of Menecrates, near the Strada Marina), and other memorials of the past ; and on a cliff overhanging the sea, behind the Casino, are the remains of a small Doric temple, with the mountain of Cardachio below it. The view from this spot is particularly beautiful, and a visit to it should by no means be omitted. It is about two miles from the town.

It is obvious from Thucydides (iii., 72) that Lake Calichiopulo is the Hyllaic harbour, and the port of Castrades 'that opposite Epirus.' As Scylax (Per. 29) mentions three ports at Corcyra, it may be presumed that the present harbour was also used in ancient times. Vido may have been the Ptychia of Thucydides, though that islet is identified by some antiquaries with the rock at the mouth of Lake Calichiopulo, and by others with the vast insulated crag on which the citadel is now built, and which was, probably, a stronghold in all ages.

Corfu is divided—for electoral purposes—into 14 districts (Demos). Lefchimo, the Southern extremity of the island, is so called from its white cliffs. All the prospects in Corfu present a union of a sea-view with a rich landscape, for the water appears everywhere interlaced with the land. The roads are excellent, and all the principal villages can be reached in a carriage ; but the varied beauties of the island cannot be thoroughly appreciated, except by those who have traced out, on horseback, some of the thousand-and-one bridle-paths which wind through the olive-groves with the freedom of mountain streams. The general absence of hedges, and of almost all show of division of property, gives the landscape a unity which is very pleasing to the eye. The olives of Corfu, it must be remembered, are not the pruned and trained fruit trees of France and Italy, but picturesque and massive forest trees ; and their pale and quivering foliage is relieved by dark groups of tall and tufted cypresses, appearing, at a little distance, like the minarets of the East, or the spires of a Gothic cathedral.

The favourite and most frequented drive, ride, and walk at Corfu, is to, what is called, the One-gun Battery (from a cannon having formerly been placed there), situated above the entrance to Lake Calichiopulo, 2½ miles South of the town, and commanding a charming prospect. In the centre of the strait below, and crowned with a wall of Byzantine architecture, is one of the islets (for there are two competitors) which claim to be the Ship of Ulysses, in allusion to the galley of the Phæanians, which, on her return from having conveyed Ulysses to Ithaca, was overtaken by the vengeance of Neptune, and changed into stone within sight of the port. (Od. xiii., 161.)

> 'Swift as the swallow sweeps the liquid way,
> The winged pinnace shot along the sea ;
> The god arrests her with a sudden stroke,
> And roots her down an everlasting rock.'

The other competitor for this honour is an isolated rock off the N.W. coast of Corfu, and which certainly, at a distance, resembles much a petrified ship in full sail. It is visible from the pass of San Pantaleone.

In the olive-groves near the Chapel of the Ascension, on the summit of a hill, about half way between the town and the One-gun Battery, is annually celebrated, on Ascension Day, a most interesting Greek festa, which the traveller should stay to see, even at the expense of some inconvenience. It will afford him an excellent opportunity of witnessing the performance of the Romaika or Pyrrhic dance, and of becoming acquainted with the picturesque costumes of the peasantry."

My readers will, I hope, forgive this long extract, but the description here given is so excellent that I have felt quite unable to curtail it.

I must now say a word about our crossing; never have I had so bad a one. A cross sea and a hurricane from the North (known here as the Bora) caught us mid-way. My Italian crew behaved splendidly, and I was more than grateful when, at 7 p.m., I could bring them to an anchor off the South shore at Gallipoli. Next morning, a change of wind made our entrance into the harbour a necessity. Yachtsmen kindly remember, that when you enter, you must come quite close round the lighthouse point (about 50 yards off the rocks), as there is very little water on the town side of the harbour. For choice, lay 80 yards from the lighthouse, with four hawsers fast to the mole 20 yards off, and one anchor ahead with 30 fathoms of chain out, or, perhaps, a little less, certainly not more, for you will have little room to weigh again, if you have much chain out and there is a strong Westerly wind. This shows how small the harbour is, but still, when you do get in, you may sleep in peace. If you command your own yacht, you will know how much this means, especially after a bad winter in Eastern waters. A better anchorage still awaits you at Cotrone, 75 miles off on your homeward-bound passage. Only last year, a magnificent breakwater was completed, behind which there is shelter enough for 50 ships and to spare. Here you can lay at single anchor in 5 or 6 fathoms of water, or haul the stern of the ship in to the shore, as you like. Do not haul in closer than from 15 to 20 yards. The water is very clear, and, if you mean to moor stern to the breakwater in this way, go on shore first and pick a spot free from all danger. In some places, you can haul in within 7 yards and have 3¼ fathoms under you; at 25 yards distance you can be sure of from 4 to 5 fathoms. There is lots of room to turn a 1,000 ton vessel, if you enter round the new mole-head, having steered S.W. for the entrance. Have nothing to do with the old port or the old mole, which lays to the Southward of the new anchorage, but enter by the North passage. Look out for the green light, and you can come in with any weather and without fear.

Now, my reader, I have done my best for you, and, if you will take a look at the photo I give of the place, you should feel quite at home, even before you enter. You are also within measurable distance of a line of rail, and within 10 minutes of a telegraph office. Capital are the fruit and vegetables, while bread and meat are quite as good here as elsewhere. If you are outward or homeward bound, to or from Corfu, you will value the two ports I have described, unless you are running all night for choice. I like to see what there is to be seen of the coast on my voyages, so my rule is to go to sea only by day, if by any means I can so arrange it.

February 24th, at 6.30, we sailed from Cotrone, and arrived, at 11.30, at Reggio, in the Straits of Messina. We were steaming with a broadside sea, which knocked us about all day, and at sunset a gale from the Southward sprang up. It would not interest the reader to detail our sufferings, but this

day will be remembered by all on board for a long
time to come. For myself, I can only say that it
was one of the worst passages I have ever made.
So dense was the fog all day, and so absolutely
necessary was it for me to make Cape Spartivento
light before entering the Straits, that my position
was not to be envied. When I did make the light, I
think I felt more relieved than I ever before remember. My Italian crew and English passengers
behaved heroically all day, and till we came to an
anchor.

Next day we crossed to Messina. Several trans-
ports were in the harbour, shipping Italian soldiers
for the African war. It rained in torrents. The
sufferings of the crowds of troops in one steamer,
and the mules in another, can be guessed. The
Italian war correspondent, who reported the spirits
of the troops as "excellent," must have been well
paid. The "mule" steamer put back twice owing to
bad weather; it was bad! A lady, whose yacht was
moored near ours, was most anxious to get to sea,
and sought my advice. I ventured the opinion that
no course could be more dangerous. The grateful
look of her Captain quite repaid me for disregarding
the fair owner's suggestion. I was thanked by both the
next morning, as that night it blew really hard, and
there was, in addition, both rain and mist. One large
steamer and a brig were lost off Cape Spartivento, in
the gale. Altogether, 20 lives were lost before sunrise
next morning. It moderated afterwards, and both
yachts went to sea. My fair neighbour went South,
we went North. At night we anchored at Palinuro.

73

An eclipse of the moon, coming on just at the time when I most wanted light, made an inshore anchorage difficult. In "rounding to" to anchor, a curious accident happened. The leadsman was in the starboard channels, and I gave the order "hard to starboard," just when he happened to have his lead line out. It fouled the screw, I never remember a similar case. We cleared it at 3 a.m., by moonlight in a calm. I happened to wake at that hour, and quietly calling up the mate and one seaman (a very clever Italian), we lowered the dinghey and did the work. The crew were much surprised and delighted in the morning when we weighed, to find everything clear. A pleasant sail brought us to Naples next day. After many tossings, and rough ones too, can anything be more restful than a peaceful sail over quiet water into Naples harbour?

Chapter XIII.

HERE is a feeling of coming home, with most lovely scenery all round you, as you enter the bright bay, which is quite indescribably delightful. How Naples has improved since I saw it first thirty-three years ago! Some trying smells remain, no doubt, but they are reduced at least two-thirds in number and one-half in intensity. The King of Italy was moving about the harbour when we arrived, seeing the troops off to Africa ; over 3,000 embarked that day. The King is popular,—the Prime Minister is not (he was). The war is hated.* Have I not heard the frantic cheers of the crowd, and the applause of the press, given in *England* to my late distinguished leader ? Then all changed, a few only remaining attached to his party, his policy, and his person ; then, again, a re-action setting in favourable to himself and his young but brilliant successor. Such is fame in England, and, I may add, elsewhere. Poor Italy ! after our own country, there is no country I love so dearly. If my reader is a yachtsman, he is probably at one with me. But to

* The reader is aware of what has happened since this was penned. The Ministry resigned after the news of the African defeat at Adowa and the Marquis of Rudini came in.

return. I have an English artillery officer as my guest. Of course he is off at once to hear and see how Italian troops, horses, guns, and ammunition are transported, and comes on board at night with notes enough to interest him and his for many a day. English yachts are here in abundance ; I think six or eight.

I go to visit my friends, Mr. and Mrs. Rendel, in their new villa. How lovely is that villa, that garden, and the private harbour with his boats anchored therein. No wonder it is the favourite resort of an Empress : it might be the home of a goddess. Venus, had she seen it, would certainly have arranged for Paris to bring Helen there. I have seen Troy,—or, rather, I have stood where Troy was,—and there is no view from that ancient city comparable to this in any way. Perhaps a fine view was not all the goddess had in her mind. My only object in writing thus in its praise is to induce my reader, when at Naples, to hire a boat, and, from off the entrance of the private harbour, to feast his eyes on the lovely grounds (seen best from the sea) and the perfect villa. This, naturally, requires no permit, and will repay the time spent.

On a previous voyage, we made use of Ponza Harbour as a night anchorage, when en route to Civita Vecchia, so we try it again ; not so successful this time. I weighed at 4 a.m., thinking I would not lose the fair wind then blowing, but before 6 a.m. the wind had drawn ahead, and a very heavy sea was getting up, so I "up helm" and ran for Gaeta. There is certainly lots of anchorage room in Gaeta, and capital shelter from almost every quarter, so, *with the lead*, you can go on boldly to the head of the bay, and anchor in whatever depth you prefer. Drawing 13 feet, I anchored in 3¼ fathoms. Capital holding ground, and lots of room to turn round there. A little far from the town no doubt, but there is not much to attract, so we do not feel the inconvenience.

Not for two days could we get away; at last we did succeed, and arrived at 11 p.m. in Civita Vecchia. If my reader should navigate his own vessel, and she is a handy one and his nerves are in good order, then try the South entrance by night,* and if you can find an anchorage *anyhow* inside till daylight, then please accept my congratulations. It is not a very simple task. We were lucky, but when, in the course of the next day, I walked on the breakwater, I hope I was duly thankful to the kind Providence that looked after us, the good helmsman at the wheel, and the very smart engineer who carried out my instructions. I remember looking over the entrance last year, and mentally resolving I never would try this port at night, but circumstances compelled me to. Next day we went to Rome, spending 24 hours there, and a very interesting day and night it was.

The Italians had then just realized the extent of their African defeat. The troops were out, and the King's Palace was guarded by the military. We walked amongst the crowds, in those parts where revolutionary tendencies were supposed to be most

---

* I would not try the North entrance by day or night. Of course, I presume that you cannot reach your harbour by day.

GAETA ENTRANCE FORT.

strongly represented. In favour of a Papa Re I heard not one cry raised. One very feeble cry for a Republic fell absolutely flat. Some Socialists were present, but they were neither strong in numbers nor coherent in their desires. There was, in short, no heart in any revolutionary party. The police moved very quietly about, and there was no fault to find with them. Italy has learnt wisdom in everything but finance; she is learning that now. She has her generals to find out too, but the material is there. I have seen, in my day, fighting men of many nations run away. I have been in two very disastrous defeats to the English arms myself, one in the Crimea, October 17th, 1854, and the other at Peiho in China. But I believe in English valour, all the same. The Italians will have their victories to follow in due course, like ourselves. I am unable to join in the cry against the Italian army. Criticism is often the most obtrusive where experience is lacking. I have yet to learn that the Italian regulars ever had a fair chance.* Time will show.

On the 7th, we sail for the Island of Elba, reaching Port Longone in the evening. The *Guinevere*, a screw schooner, started just after us, and got in 10 minutes before us; we were together all day. She is a much larger and more powerful vessel, and we were very proud at doing so well.

March 9th, our last day's sail. We weighed early, and reached Leghorn about 2 p.m. I had previously written to the English Consul, asking him

---

* It has since been abundantly proved that some of the finest deeds of valour ever known were done on that fatal Adowa day.

kindly to obtain leave from the Italian Naval Authorities for me to enter the inner port at once, and have the gates opened on my arrival. Nothing could surpass the kindness of the officials, who had the bridge gates opened for us as we came in, so at once, we moored the yacht 'for the summer inside the basin, and made arrangements for storing her gear.

Wintering or summering in an Italian port differs widely from the same operation in England. In England, if you want a new boiler or great changes made in your machinery, you will find everything ready to your hand, and, if your purse is an ample one, nothing can be more perfect than the arrangements which any of the leading firms in Cowes or Southampton will make for you. If, however, economy in repairs, or the price of your berth and store-room be any object, I should be doing an injustice to those who have behaved very well to me, if I did not state that, having tried England and Italy, I have found Italy suits my purse and my temper the best. It would, however, be an injustice to the English firms if I did not state, that for rapidity of work, as well as for the ease with which a contract can be made, England stand first. Yes, and a long way first.

Chapter XIV.

 PROMISED in my last work (to which I have previously referred) to give the readers of my next book the result of my inquiries as regards English and Foreign crews. I much regret that, owing probably to the very bad weather we all experienced in the East of the Mediterranean during the winter, very few yachts were out, and, therefore, whatever information I may give, must be taken only as being founded on the best evidence I could obtain, and which I could not myself regard as conclusive. So far as I am concerned, I consider I am in a position to speak almost conclusively, but it would be a gross injustice to those who may hold opposite views, did I not make the above admission.

As regards the comfort of the owner, and certainly the crew have very much to do with this, Italians will bear very favourable comparison with Englishmen. They never get drunk or break their leave, they are easily pleased, and work far more steadily at daily routine work than Englishmen. Twice in my cruise I ordered steam at 6 a.m., but waking myself at 2 a.m., and finding a clear moon and favourable change of weather, I called the men and I was off.

On neither occasion did I hear one word of complaint. Of course, either you, if you command your own vessel, or your Captain if you do not, must speak Italian. This goes without saying. Italians are cheaper as regards wages, and much less extortionate in every way. On the other hand, the English sailor is far better for boat-work. He also dresses much smarter. I fancy, too, he stands the cold better, but I am far from being quite clear on this point. I am assured, that in heavy weather Jack is the better man of the two, but my experience makes me somewhat doubtful on this point, as far as yachts are concerned. I admit, that on board a man-of-war, where you have naval discipline, the Englishman comes out far ahead in almost every particular, but, for Mediterranean yachting, give me an Italian crew. I would not even try a Spanish or a Greek one; I plead my bigotry and insular prejudice for not writing about them.

I have heard from French yachting friends very good accounts of their men, but old feuds and prejudices, and rivalries, would, I imagine, make it very difficult for English owners to work smoothly with them. French cooks, however, are often beyond praise, and in this capacity, as every one knows, our neighbours far surpass all rivals.

Russians are often capital engineers, most painstaking, and very proud of their engines and their own work on them ; I have proved this. They are good linguists, too, and can generally speak three or four languages ; a most useful qualification on board any yacht, or elsewhere. Speaking of languages, I hope my reader will forgive me for mentioning a fact he may have overlooked, viz., that sailor's French and Parisian French are not the same by any means. I once remember an English friend of mine being much confused by this discovery. He would have been considered, for an Englishman, quite a first-class French scholar in Paris. At Marseilles, he had to speak very slowly indeed, and with much gesticulation, to make himself understood when conversing with a native seaman. A similar hint may not be out of place in regard to different Italian dialects. I was much amused by finding that my Genoa and Leghorn seamen were often quite unable to understand their Neapolitan countrymen; but, of course, this is a very extreme case. Generally speaking, good Italian is understood all over Italy; though a good Italian scholar will often find that he is almost unable to understand what a Neapolitan is saying to him. On board Mediterranean yachts with foreign crews, there are usually many Italian seaman who habitually use certain English naval expressions:— "Starboard," "Port," "Steady," "Ahead," "Astern," "Stop," "Let go," and "Make fast," are all familiar terms in constant use, to which they are accustomed.

One great blessing one enjoys with Italian North country seamen, is that they are extraordinarily cleanly in their habits. They really seem to be always washing their clothes. The best way to ship such a crew, should my reader desire to do so, is to apply at the English Consulate some weeks before they are required, and there he will generally find some one who will engage seamen for him at about

G

5*s*. a head commission. This plan has many advantages over any other. There are always interpreters, commission agents, old captains, and hangers on of all sorts, who will offer their help. Employ none of these. It may not be out of place here to mention, that all engagements are made in Italian lire, of which, as a rule, 27 go to the English pound. The quoted price can be, of course, seen in the papers daily. The usual wage for an A.B. is 25 lire a week, with one more added, if he is coxwain of a boat or oilman.

Italian carpenters and shipwrights are far handier and better than our English ones (so far, at least, as my own experience goes), indeed, they seem able, and, what is more, are willing to do almost anything. Their wages are about 30 lire a week, and they are worth it. Firemen are at about 27 to 33 lire, according to their experience and ability. I strongly recommend, however, English stewards, for every possible reason.

Uniforms, of any desired pattern, can be made, or, rather, copied, by Italian tailors. You will do wisely, when fitting out, to order also, *in addition*, a warm jersey to each man. For some reason or another, Italians seem more chilly than Englishmen, but of this I cannot be sure. Little considerations like these affecting their comforts, are, however, very highly appreciated by Italians, and will repay the owner. One great advantage in an Italian crew, is the hold the Captain has over his men in one important respect. Every Italian seaman is obliged to have in his own possession when on shore, and his Captain's when afloat, a book which contains his date of birth, his certificates, and, indeed, all about himself. This is the law. On joining, he gives this up to his Captain, who is in legal charge of it till he leaves. The seaman then adds his late discharge to former documents, when he is again ready to show his papers to his next employer, or to the police, if required. The advantage of this arrangement to every *good* man, as well as to his employer, is obvious. If a bad man, and he should desert, the police would soon find him on shore, and he would be prosecuted as a seaman without his book, as well as a deserter; so Italians do not desert. If he misbehaves, his certificates show this, and it is against him in getting another ship, so he does not misbehave or get drunk. I can conceive no arrangement better calculated to separate the bad from the good. To prevent the capricious use of this power by the Captain, the seaman has a right to demand a court from the Consul, to inquire into his own or his Captain's conduct. The Consul must, of course, be satisfied that the case is one which requires a court, or the Consul may be able to settle the case himself at once. In every case, the seaman has quite sufficient protection against any abuse of power. Could the same, or some similar arrangement, be carried out in England, there would be no necessity for English owners to look elsewhere for their seamen.

In Austria, yachts belonging to their Royal Yacht Squadron ship their crews from the Royal Austrian Navy, who are engaged under terms which are advantageous both to the country and the owner, while a place on board a yacht is much sought after by every Austrian seaman.* It has always been a source of astonishment to me, why a mixed Committee of well-known practical yachtsmen and Naval Officers should not be appointed, to report to Parliament on the whole question of the employment of seamen on board yachts, with a view to their being drilled at convenient times, and subject to service in the Royal Navy, if called upon. The Regulations existing, bearing on this point require revision. I think, now, I have done all that I can to impress upon my reader the importance of the subject. I will now give him my experience in regard to another.

We will leave the question of the yacht's crew, and come to the vessel herself. My vessel was painted black, she is now white, or, rather, she is painted so pale a grey that she almost looks white. White yachts are no doubt increasing in number, and this will show that, for various reasons, owners and Captains prefer it. I will give my reasons for the change I have made. Let me admit at once that these will not, perhaps, seem quite conclusive, but the weight of evidence, such as it is, seemed to indicate the desirability of change. I am very frequently at sea, and lay in harbour, generally, only for short periods. My vessel looks presentable always after one day in harbour, no matter what the weather; when she was painted black it took two days to get her to look as well; so it appeared, and appears still

---

* Some little difficulty has lately arisen, in regard to the employment of Austrian Naval Officers with their men, but the question is, I am assured, one which will shortly be amicably arranged.

to me. You can neither patch black or white satis-
factorily, but, if you must do one or the other, to my
fancy the white looks less bad than the black. Italian
paints, I may here remark, are remarkably good and
cheap. Lastly, white paint keeps the vessel *much*
cooler when the sun is out. A friend of mine, who
still paints his yacht black, has urged against my
objection that his ship looks better so, that she
always was painted black (a very conservative argument), and, lastly, that his crew, when in harbour,
always got into trouble if not employed, and it keeps
them busy. The last argument I feel I am unable
to meet, so I am silent, and our friendship remains.
We had bad weather enough this winter to give our
grey paint a severe trial.

Chapter XV.

Y reader will have gathered from the foregoing pages, that the weather we experienced was decidedly bad; but, from inquiries I have made, I believe it was exceptionally bad. There have, no doubt, been bad years from time to time, but then there have been good ones, and these seem to be in the proportion of about two to one. Again, in the winter months, Athens and Constantinople have very different climates; Athens nearly always being the best. The harbours, also, on the home side of Athens, are far more numerous and better than they are on the other side, and, if the yachtsman will bear in mind the water difficulty I have before drawn attention to in the district of the Piræus, there is no reason why he should not enjoy himself immensely as far North as Syra. If you go farther North, you must expect less and less comfort, and less and less warmth. It is very difficult, also, for the stranger to realize how hard it can blow *down* on vessels at anchor in all the Eastern basin of the Mediterranean and the Ægean Sea. You may be anchored behind a hill which rises almost perpendicularly from the harbour, but gusts of wind come down this elevation with a force which must be felt to be realized. The only squalls like these that I know of in England are the gusts that descend from Mount Edgecumbe at Plymouth; and they exhibit only very poor examples of how it can blow in the East. Whenever I moored to the shore in Eastern waters, I used two hemp and two wire hawsers, and was' always thankful I had done so. Of course my experience was only during the winter months, when bad weather is to be looked for. In the advanced spring, summer, and autumn, my friends tell me that these squalls are very rare, and never blow either so hard or for so long. The barometer no doubt, on the Southern side of the Dardanelles, will almost always give some indication of coming weather, but it wants watching very closely. Between the entrance of the Dardanelles and Constantinople, the glass is of no use at all, but I am assured by Captains of Black Sea steamers that the barometer there during the winter months can be fairly trusted. It works, however, they say, in this region, in a contrary way, as a rising glass means bad weather, and a falling glass means good weather. I am inclined to believe this to be true, as I certainly saw signs of it at Constantinople.

I confess to a feeling of depression while writing about these waters, and for this reason:—That I do not believe all the nautical writers in the world could make these ports popular with yachtsmen during the winter months. There is really too much to put up with, and too little return. Of course, if the traveller is on shooting bent, he will find in parts of Asia Minor all he wants, but the state of the country is such, that, unless he has really first-class information from some English Consul, some English resident, engineer, or trader, it will be wise for him to postpone his visit until his information is more complete.

In my last work, I gave cyclists all the information I could in regard to their favourite pastime. I can now put all the information I possess, in regard to roads between the Piræus and Constantinople, in a very few lines. A bicycle takes up very little room on any yacht, but to take one on board, if you are cruising in these Eastern waters, is really to waste useful space. North and East of the Piræus, your bicycle will be of no use to you. An old saddle and bridle you will often find useful, and, if you have ladies on board, a lady's saddle will prove quite a luxury. On many of the islands, and on the main land, there are almost always ponies, mules, or donkeys you can hire, and if you can induce these animals to put up with an English saddle, you will save yourself much discomfort. In regard to guns and cartridges, no one who has not experienced it would believe how hard it is to get these simple requirements out from England, and on board your yacht. They seem never to arrive if sent out by steamer, indeed many Companies will not carry cartridges at all at any price, and then those who do charge so highly for freight that it is almost ruinous. Of course you cannot send them overland. If your yacht is in the Mediterranean, the best thing you can do is send them out to some English port, such as Malta or Gibraltar, at least six weeks before they will be required. Get some friend or agent at one of these places to take care of them for you till you call

ENTRANCE TO TEMPLE OF JUPITER, ATHENS.

for them, and shut your eyes and ears to the expense. This will be heavy, but it will be nothing to what you will have to pay if they go to a foreign port. All foreign powers are jealous of the shipment and landing of arms, and the excise duties on these goods in France and Italy are enormous. Many years will have to pass before the powers that be become aware that the invasion of their country would not be made with small shot or smooth bore guns, and that the importation of the latest improvements in fire arms into their country would be an immense boon to their own gun-makers, through whose hands many of them would pass, and to whom they would be sent for repairs. It is curious to note in one's conversations with French and Italian gentlemen, how, without exception, they see and admit this, yet the wisdom of the café, of the railway carriage, and of the pavement, will not enter the bureau for years. Surely it was one of England's wisest Statesmen who, years ago, saw how important it was that foreign war ships should be built in England, and foreign guns and rifles should be manufactured here. The English manufacturer is thus always up to date. The weak retort that these might some day be used against us is now only used by those who are ill-informed of the advantage gained, and cannot, therefore, weigh both sides. In these matters, there is no such thing as an unmixed advantage.

In regard to duties, as I am on the subject, I think the yachtsman should know how many disadvantages he will have to contend against in regard to what used to be called "medical comforts." Of course, in very large ports, such as Nice, he would probably be able to procure any patent or other medicine he requires, but, as he proceeds Eastwards in the Mediterranean, his difficulties will increase. So many of our English patent medicines are in common use to-day, and the facilities of getting them out from England are so great, that possibly he will forgive me for reminding him of how necessary it is to be well provided in this respect. At Naples and Corfu he *may* find what he wants, if the medicine he seeks is really well known, but East of these ports he will find it very hard to find anything he wants. I may, however, mention a fact which will be useful to him. There are in all these Eastern towns an increasing number of able medical men, whose knowledge of the requirements of their districts is often very useful. A knowledge of the peculiarities of English constitutions is lacking, but each English vessel that requires attendance increases this knowledge. A drug or patent medicine may, again, have suited well in other climates, while its action here is not so favourable. I have myself found that sometimes, when I had a chance of consulting physicians holding French or German diplomas (there are very few holding English), that they have been able often to substitute something very suitable to the climate in which they live. At Corfu, the doctor of the port is one of those who hold a French Diploma, I have had to consult him in regard both to my passengers and crew, and always with advantage. The English Consul or Vice-Consul is almost always able to give good advice as to who to go to, at almost every port. The charges are usually very moderate, and I am bound to say, that the medical men whom I have had to consult, in regard either to myself, my crew, or my passengers, have all been kind, reasonable in their charges, and attentive. It often happens, also, that an English vessel with a doctor on board visits the same port you are in, and, in case of necessity, a little diplomacy will often procure his services. I have, however, sometimes discovered, that if the great authority consulted finds out that you are employing a doctor with a French or German diploma, he proceeds to differ with him forthwith. Perhaps that is innate in the British character, and not even a first-class medical training can quite extinguish the hereditary taint. There is this difficulty, also, with the English doctor, viz., that he may possibly pre-scribe something the chemist has not got, or, if he has, its preparation is not the same in all countries. Colds and coughs are, I think, the most common maladies which crew and passengers suffer from during the winter, and these are not usually difficult to cure. I am certainly no physician, but I fancy both these complaints get well on board ship more quickly than on shore, provided a few good nights' rest can be secured, in any case, my own ailments of this description got well very soon at sea.

Would my reader care for some information as to food in Eastern waters? Certainly, what may be called the daily requisites of life can very easily be obtained in most ports, except cow's milk, butter, and cocoa. Goat's milk can almost always be obtained, but good cow's milk and butter you must say good-bye to, when quitting the Gulf of Corinth. My steward bought some at Athens, Syra, and Constantinople, but it was very poor in quality, and quite double the price usually paid in England. In the French Stores, at the Pera Palace Hotel in Constantinople, I bought some beautiful butter in 2 lb. and 4 lb. tins. This will keep fresh for almost any time, if kept in a cool place. The same may be said of the tinned cream, which is more like Devonshire cream than anything else. We bought enough of both these commodities to last us three months, and it kept good all the time. Tea and cream can be got good at these stores, but the price, owing to the duty, is heavy indeed. Curiously enough, we got here also, some real York hams ; I think the best I have ever tasted, and at quite a fair price. I have mentioned these stores before, but I make no apology for again drawing attention to them, because this is the only spot East of Malta where provisions of this description, and of surpassing excellence, can be obtained. In view of the coming revival of the Olympic games, efforts are being made at Athens to set up stores, or, rather, to replenish existing stores with these and other requisites, but the very heavy duties (much heavier there than at Constantinople for most goods) will, I fear, handicap that City for some time to come. However, if they can be got at all, and at any price, it will be a great boon to the touring and yachting community. Some day it will occur to a Greek Chancellor of the Exchequer, that if he can put his hands into the pockets of three men, and pull out a shilling from

VOSTITZA HARBOUR, GULF OF CORINTH.

52 A

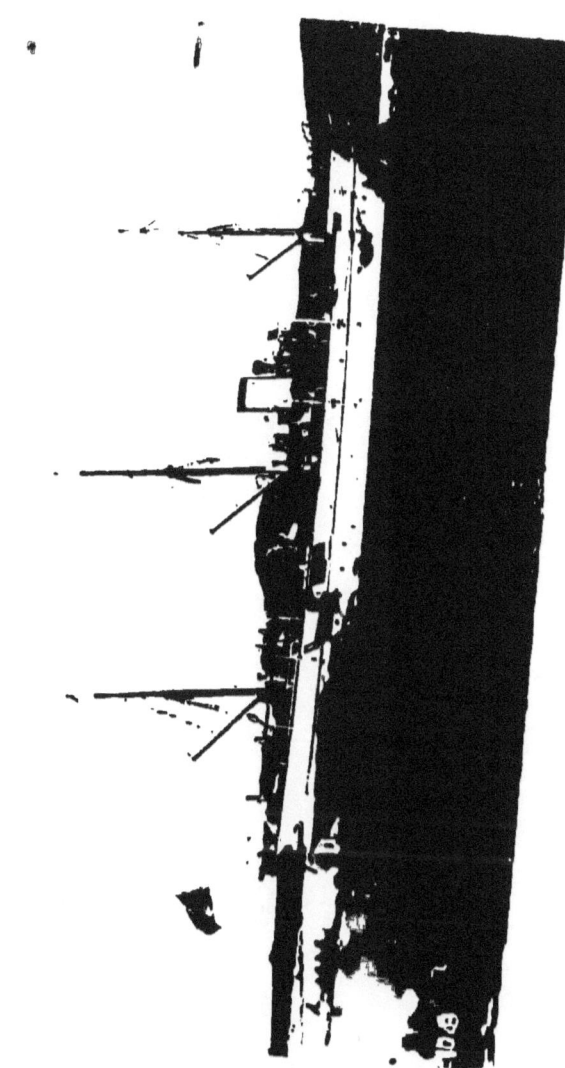

RUSSIAN CRUISER.

each, he will be better off than if able only to put his hands into one man's pocket, and from thence extract two shillings. But this enlightenment is far off and quite in the dim distance, so we need not discuss it further.

Of daily provisions, such as bread, meat, chickens, eggs, vegetables, and fruit, I found no difficulty anywhere in obtaining these. Bread is not only good in all towns East of the Gulf of Corinth, but in many it is quite remarkable for its purity and excellence. In the small villages it is coarse and bad, but one is seldom compelled to buy this. The price of bread is, if anything, cheaper than in England of the same quality. Meat is cheap in Greek quarters, and is fairly good; it is *very* cheap, and much better usually, in Turkish towns and Turkish islands. My steward has often bought the best beef and mutton at about 5*d.* the lb. I have seen at Chanak, in the Dardanelles, really very good beef and mutton at about 4*d.* a pound. At this port, I bought three fine hares, four wild ducks, and eight woodcocks for 15 francs, not a bad bargain. At Gallipoli (in Turkey), a boat well laden with game would often go alongside a steamer bound for Constantinople, and, if the owner of the boat did not sell off, he would then come alongside of our yacht, and it was really quite wonderful how cheaply he would then part with the remainder. In none of the islands, Turkish or Greek, can meat be bought more cheaply than here, also, when in season, partridges, and, indeed, almost every sort of game, can be procured in great abundance. Chickens and eggs are also very cheap and very good in all places where they can be bought at all, and there are very few places where they cannot be bought.

In the very small islands I have, however, sometimes found that, so far from having provisions to sell, the inhabitants were anxious to buy. They depend very largely on their fishing boats and small coasting schooners to bring their provisions from the main land, but if the prevailing gales have been so heavy that these could not put to sea, they are often hard pressed.

Vegetables are excellent, abundant, and cheap, almost everywhere, and, if you are fortunate enough to call in anywhere where the market has not been spoilt, you will have every reason to be satisfied with what you get, and pleased with the bill. Fruit is abundant, no doubt, but here a word of warning may not be out of place. It often happens that you wish to go to sea at daylight or soon after, and your caterer or steward has, the evening before, ordered everything to be ready for him in the early morning. He knows you want to be off, and he does not wish to keep you waiting, so he takes unripe oranges and fruit to sea, having had no time to look these carefully over. I found the best way in the East was only to buy fruit when there was lots of time, even at the risk of having sometimes to go without. You may be wise enough not to eat unripe fruit, but your steward, rather than see it wasted, turns it over to the men; then you may be delayed at your next port for two or three days, till the crew have got over it. This is an indiscretion which my sailors sometimes indulged in. When an Italian is ill, he is very ill, and it seems

VIEW OF ACROPOLIS, FROM ENTRANCE TO STADION.

to me that, when he recovers, he always regards it as more or less of a miracle, and seems quite surprised.

Apropos of catering, if you have a Greek on board, he can certainly buy provisions, or indeed anything, at half the price you can, so it is quite worth while shipping one. At Ithaca, some capital firemen can be got, and should you ship one, he will pay his own wages over and over again, if you send him ashore with your steward or caterer. Why there should be good fireman in Ithaca has surprised many, as it surprised me when I first heard of it, but, as a matter of fact, many of the Danube steamers get their fire-men from there. I shipped one, and found my other fireman only too gladly did his work, when he found out how much he gave the crew to eat, and how little he paid for it. It saved so much quarrelling, both on shore and on board, that I hope I may be pardoned for mentioning the fact.

We have now done with food, so our next con-sideration is wine. My heart fails me when I enter on this most disputable ground. My publisher tells me that, in a very short time, some 600 persons bought my first book. Will the same number buy this one? If so, am I to risk making 600 unrelenting enemies for the rest of my days? You may lend a gun to a friend, and you may know its little failing to be that cartridges somehow always jam in that gun. You may lend another friend a hunter that no living man can get over a water jump. For all these, and worse things, shall you be forgiven, *in time,* but be the means of pouring a bad bottle of wine down his throat, and you shall never be forgiven, nay, more the heinousness of your crime increases as years go on, each dinner party affording an opportunity of recalling the circumstance. In one of the countries with which I am acquainted, there lives a gentleman of undoubted ability who has obtained Cabinet rank. He is unpopular all the same, and, curiously enough, he has never been able to account for his unpopularity. I have had the honour of being asked to his table twice, and went once. A colleague of his, in conversation with me quite lately, remembered a dinner he had eaten at his house three years ago. His host had committed the unpardonable crime. I must see if I can avoid it.

"What wine does the landlord drink?" has often in England been the question which has saved many a man from a bad headache. It would not do so in the East. There is a tartness about most of the red, and even a few of the white wines, grown in Greece, which I can never get over. My rule, however, is almost always to drink white wine. In Italy, Vino Capri, when it can be got old, is the best wine I know of. I always drink it. At Corfu and Ithaca, really good white wine can be got. At the former place, I drink Domestica, and at the latter there is a native wine 17 years old, sold by a merchant who speaks capital English, and who lives near the Pratique Office. I always lay in a store of this, and I drink nothing else for lunch or dinner till my stock is finished. All my friends like it too. As he is the only man who sells wine of this age, and speaks English, you cannot make a mistake. The corks of the bottles should be seen to, as it is drawn from the cask and bottled on the spot.

At Patras there is some capital wine sold by a German merchant, who has a large store; it is well worth a visit, and about three miles out of the town. You can get wine 5, or even 6 years old there; they have, however, some which I tasted 8 years old, but they would not sell that, so I went without. Perhaps my reader may have better luck. At Athens, at the large hotels, there is some very good wine. Talk privately to the manager first before ordering, then note the name of the wine and merchant on the label, and order from him direct, *after having sampled in his own office.* In comparison to the prices we pay in England for good wines, all the above will seem cheap.

At Syra there is a little good wine, but it is almost all in private cellars. At Constantinople, there is no wine you are likely to want that you cannot get. Inquire from the very courteous managers of either the "Bristol" or "Pera Palace" Hotels. Perhaps my taste is not a highly refined one, but I confess to a partiality for these light country wines, grown on the Southern slopes of the main land in Greece and Turkey. They give me no headache, and are void of acidity, that is when I can get them fairly old, and, of course, of the finest growth.

Real old whiskey, worthy of the name, is now so popular, that I must risk the chance of being thought tedious if I say a word about this drink. Not all the hotel proprietors put together, between Malta and Constantinople, should induce me to depart from my custom of securing this beverage in either England or Scotland. I should, however, feel quite culpable,

H

did I say a word to discourage them in their efforts to give of their best to their customers; all the more so, as I know both the demand for the very best, and the supply, is better year by year.

To those who prefer brandy, I may say that, in two or three years, lovers of this spirit will find a genuine, purely made liquid bearing this name, which will *then* be 8 or 9 years old, ready for sale at Athens. The same is also true of Cephalonia. In both these localities, a determination has been shown to endeavour to rival the French in this manufacture. To my mind and taste, the Frenchman comes in first up to the moment of writing, but I am far from clear that the future should be, or could be, guaranteed to him. I would still, if going East, call in at Nice, or some French port, to secure a supply of this commodity, if I thought there was likely to be any demand for it on board.

Of the class of drinks known as non-intoxicants, a few are advertised in the larger hotels at Athens and Constantinople, but only there. I had not the privilege of meeting any one who had tried these, and I did not myself feel disposed, so I fear I cannot help my reader in this respect. Of mineral waters, to take with wine or spirits, I tried a few; all good. That is to say, all were good that happened to be well corked, and only a very few were not.

Another subject, and a very homely one now, demands attention. "It is time we had our washing done, sir," says the steward. "I can only last three days more," says your lady or gentleman guest; so this question must be faced. In no part of the

Mediterranean is it possible to have your clothes more frequently washed than in these Eastern waters, and, I may add, in no part do your clothes suffer more under the operation. The moment you come to an anchor anywhere, you will find amongst the many commodities offered you by the agents or interpreters who flock on board, a very large number who will take your washing on shore there and then, and offer to return it in two days. On two separate occasions, they kept their word literally, but the washing came back wet and unstarched. Oh those agents ! The washing of clothes is more often than not, one of the yachtsman's severest trials. Not only does it very frequently happen that you are bound to stay in harbour when a fair breeze springs up, but, when your washing does come on board, many a garment that was landed a shirt comes on board a rag. The usual price being about 3 francs a dozen, you have made your contract, or, more probably, your steward has for you. To your surprise, your washerman charges much more,—why ? He has counted each sock as one piece, while one exceptional rascal had the impudence to charge for each shirt, each collar, and each cuff; the collars and cuffs being parts of the shirt, and sewn on. Such are some of their many little tricks. The best way of all is to make inquiries, before sending washing on shore, of that tradesman with whom you have your largest dealings,—the Consul (if a friend), or the first respectable man you meet. If there is a large hotel near, then pay the extra $\frac{1}{2}$-franc a dozen, and send your washing there, it will pay you.

Now in regard to coaling, just a few words. How often does my reader think that he really has on board the amount of coal charged for in the bill he so readily pays? I know, on the best authority, how small is the proportion of yachts that achieve this; I mean where no person gets a secret commission, when the baskets contain the coal they are supposed to, or where the boat sent off to the yacht really has on board the number of tons ordered, and which very certainly will be charged for in the bill. I should not have alluded to this, had it not been that I have experienced in a small way, what some of my friends have in a much larger. The Greek coal merchant is, I fear, by no means necessarily an immaculate person. That the fault does not always, or even primarily lay with the merchant, I am well aware. There are, unfortunately, too many yacht owners who know where the fault *does* lay, but, either they fail to get absolute proof, and are therefore well advised in not bringing a charge, or they think the trouble of sifting the matter too great; or they know that either A. or B., perhaps both, always expect and get a commission (the owner little dreams how much) or, having made up their minds to spend so much on their cruise, do not very much care whether they have to lay their vessel up a week or two sooner or later. In a great number of cases, the owner, though he hates being done, does not want to be bothered, and stops, so to speak, at the half-way house, where he just finds out enough to annoy him, but does not take the trouble to run the dishonesty home, and stop it. Perhaps he cannot.

REGGIO ANCHORAGE.

Chapter XVI.

" HAT are we to do ? " said an old yachting skipper to me one day, "our employment is the most precarious in the world. We have no pensions to look forward to, the children at home want something to eat, and the Governor does not seem to mind : what's a sovereign or two to him ? why, about as much as a shilling to me ! and he'd a deal sooner not be bothered." I confess there is now no answer to this, but when the mixed Committee of naval officers and yacht owners, which I have suggested, meet and send in their report, there should be an answer. Yachting captains will then have pensions, for they will be old naval men, and the path of honesty will be made much easier for them. "Five and twenty years ago, sir, I entered as a boy on board H.M.S. *Progress*, and now I command one of the finest yachts out of Cowes." This should not be an impossible boast. Surely of all employments for pensioned seamen or petty officers, none could suit them better than an officer's place on board a yacht. Yet there are two drawbacks. One his want of

navigating knowledge, and the other the vast differ-
ence between yacht and man-of-war service. This,
however, would be somewhat remedied if the seamen of yachts were, for the most part, naval reserve
men; while the privilege of studying navigation, free
of cost, on board Her Majesty's ships, with a view
to future employment on board yachts and merchant
vessels, would, it seems to me, be an inducement to
boys to enter our Navy. I would suggest that,
whenever any petty officer desired to study navigation, he might be granted facilities for so doing, if his
Captain approved. The sight of a yacht's Captain in
the uniform of the R.Y.S., or any recognised yacht
club, wearing also a distinguished mark, showing that
he belonged to some class of naval reserve officers, or
petty officers, would, I conceive, be a great inducement
to English boys to enter the Royal Navy. Yachts go
everywhere now, and each qualified yacht Captain
might have powers, under proper conditions, to send
boys for enlistment in the service. Of course, they
must be encouraged to do so. The position of a
qualified yacht Captain would then be an enviable
one. I am quite unable to see who the person could
be who would not gain by such an arrangement.
The State obviously would, for there would be further
inducement to enlist. The yacht owner, even if not
a seaman, would be quite capable of appreciating the
obvious advantage of having a well tried class of
men to choose from; the men selected as Captains
and Officers would gain, and the boys of England
would gain; one more opening for them.

"I suppose, Sir, I should not be expected to put

my hands in the slush bucket?" said a candidate,
who lately sought the position of Captain of one of
the R.Y.S. yachts. The owner had been an old
naval officer, and his reply was significant. "Oh
dear no," he said, "I *often* did, to get the tar off *my*
hands after going aloft, or after showing someone
how to knot or splice, but, of course, I should not
expect you to do so." The yacht Captain of the
future, as I hope he may be, would be much amused
at any friend of his asking for such an exemption.

I should be very sorry if my reader should suppose
by any of these remarks, that I am unaware of how
many excellent yacht Captains there are now afloat,
who readily turn their hands to any work, who are
not to be bribed by any one, and whose value to
their employer is proved from the fact that they are
not only engaged, year after year, for sea service, but
are often retained when the vessel is laid up, and
when the work to be done on board is not of an
arduous character. My only object in writing as I
have done, is, if possible, to suggest improvements in
our present practice where improvement is felt to be
necessary, and to sound a note of warning to those
who may be sailing in Eastern waters for the first
time, in regard to their dealings with merchants and
others with whom they may be brought in contact.

I make no apology for following up my remarks in
regard to coal, with a word or two about water.
Every yacht captain sees, or ought to see, that his
tanks are thoroughly cleaned out at least once (they
should be twice) every year. While I was in the
East, I had my own looked to twice in five months,

and I did not think the trouble too great or the precaution by any means unnecessary. Of course, if you could make sure of always watering either at Syra, Patras, or Poros Island, this precaution would be superfluous. But, unless you carry a large supply of fresh water or condense your own water on board, you will often have to trust to good luck in getting a perfectly pure fluid brought off, and this, of course, in an absolutely clean boat or tank. I am sorry to say that you have only good luck to trust to, and, after rainy weather, you will be indeed fortunate, if the discoloured water which is brought alongside is, nevertheless, quite wholesome and fit to drink. When this happened to me, I always pumped overboard all the water I had left in the tanks, cleaned them as well as I could, and then pumped in fresh water at the first good watering place I reached, using the discoloured water only for the passage, and always after boiling. Filters are useful on board at all times, if they are kept clean, and well looked after, but perhaps there is no part of the Mediterranean where this precaution is more needed than in its Eastern portion. As regards price, in 9 cases out of 10, you are at first asked a much larger sum than is right or usual. I have been asked 7 francs a ton, when 4 francs has been eventually accepted; I have paid as little as 3 Greek francs (about 1s. 6d.), and as much as 5 Italian lire (about 4s.) a ton, never more. In every place the price varies, and in the same place it again varies at different times of the year, and according to the demand. I am very sorry I cannot be of more assistance to my reader in this respect. One hint, however, I may give which might prove of use. If, on your outward jonrney, a list of prices paid is accurately kept, it will be found of great value for the return journey. It saved me a great deal of argument when I could state, "this is what I paid before."

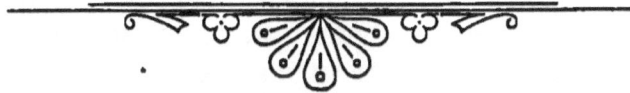

Chapter XVII.

S regards air and climate:—The air on the shores of Asia Minor where the ground is flat and marshy, is really as bad as can be, but then the sport to be obtained is often really good, and, as the evening draws in and the sportsman grows weary, the noxious vapours rise, and then "quinine quick," or you are in for a fever. Even with every precaution there is some danger. This risk, however, decreases with the arrival of frost or snow, so the winter is, doubtless, the safest time, even though the most disagreeable. I have no fault, on the contrary, nothing but praise, for the air of the Piræus, and, indeed, the whole of the mountainous or sandy East, right up to Constantinople. I have heard a few complaints of the air of Smyrna, it being regarded by some as rather relaxing, but the weather was so cold while we were there that we did not feel this. I suppose the truth really is that in almost all hot climates, and in the warm months, the air is relaxing, and *vice versâ* in the winter. The breezes off and on to the Greek Islands, during the Spring and Autumn, are described by all residents as bracing and delightful, which I quite believe. The

ISLANDS BETWEEN ÆGINA AND POROS.

number of villas and residences of all sorts, up and down the Gulf of Corinth, are, in themselves, quite a good enough test of the value the inhabitants attach to the air and climate of that locality. Taken as a whole, there is little fault to be found with the climate in Eastern waters, except for the three winter months, when I am told by medical men that, persons with delicate chests or unusually subject to cold, had better postpone their visits till the spring.

Every one is acquainted, either actually or by report, with what is known as Mediterranean fever, so I need say little about it. In the case of a young naval officer of my acquaintance, who used to suffer much from it, a return to the station was absolutely forbidden. Doctors say that no one should return to the Mediterranean, who has once had a bad attack. I know nothing more disappointing than to see a fine able bodied young man struggling, while still in the Mediterranean, to get over this liability to attack and failing each time. He comes home at last, and is then sent to China or some other station which is, perhaps, considered a worse one, and he then finds himself, much to his own astonishment, in excellent health and as strong as any one. So after Mediterranean fever come home. That almost all Italians, Greeks, and Turks wear something warm round their waists, seems enough in itself to show the necessity of not forgetting some such protection. I mention this purposely, as in England this is not a regular practice. The Lenten fast, also, which in Catholic and Greek orthodox countries is kept with more or less strictness, has undoubtedly a very favourable effect on the health, and at a time of year when a change of food seems called for. I have known English doctors, resident in Italy, who always recommend something of the sort to their patients, quite apart, of course, from any religious motive. On board yachts which are much at sea, and wherever much hard work has to be done, other considerations naturally arise; but diet, in any case, in spring and autumn, has I fancy, in the Mediterranean, to be always carefully watched by delicate persons.

I have, I hope, laid before my reader most of the points which generally influence yachtsmen in the choice of where to go. Should any tourist now determine to try Eastern waters, he will, I fancy, at most seasons of the year be far from disappointed, although, of course, luxuries which he has been accustomed to and obtained easily in ports such as Nice, Algiers, or Naples, will be denied him. He will, of course, also wish to keep alive a recollection of the places he visits, so he will make purchases. How is he to send these home? I will tell him a little further on. At almost every port in the Ægean Sea and the Sea of Marmora, and along the coast of Asia Minor, he will be offered ancient (?) coins, either by persons who come alongside, or when he goes on shore. I bought 40 coins once at Foujes for 10 francs. Two of these were really of some value, perhaps about 5 or 6 francs each. It was a very happy bargain, the result of an accident I am sure. But men mark the hits and not the misses, and

CAPE COLONNA, GULF OF ATHENS.

109

I could tell some tales with a bearing of different complexion. A knowledge of coins is, I conceive, a rare accomplishment, or else I am not fortunate in knowing many persons who are good judges. The best way to buy valuable coins, should there exist such a desire, is, I think, to confine purchases to the larger towns, unless in very exceptional instances. If this is done, and some known judge or expert is employed (the best hotel keepers often know these), then a prize or two may be secured. Of course, now and then the peasantry who first find them may not have the power of discovering the value of the coins they possess, and you may have the luck to pick up a bargain, without yourself knowing that you are under-paying the poor man. But this piece of luck happens to few, and I suspect that if a man desires a souvenir of his trip, or wishes to make a present to a friend, he generally would prefer paying a good round sum and securing a really valuable specimen, to any chance methods.

As an exception to the advice I have ventured (not without some misgivings) to offer, in regard to purchases only in the larger towns, on account of the comparative ease with which experts can there be found, I may mention that, in Chios there lives an agreeable and highly educated gentleman, who is also a great authority on coins. He is in constant correspondence with the British Museum on this subject, and is an expert of very high standing. I purposely do not mention his name, as I should be repaying his kindness to me in very base coin indeed, if, in consequence of the publicity I gave him, he became

troubled with letters which might cause him annoyance; but I think I might say this, that if any
yachtsman who was anchoring off this island on his
way, perhaps, to Smyrna, were to call on the British
Vice-Consul and receive an introduction from him,
the visit might prove not only interesting but in-
structive. As souvenirs, of course gold coins are
more in request than silver; but the demand is a
very long way ahead of the supply. Gold orna-
ments, of very ancient date, may here and there be
obtained, but the prices asked, as may be imagined,
are high indeed. Should my reader make the acquaintance of any of our Consuls or Vice-Consuls in
Asia Minor, particularly in the neighbourhood of
Troy, Ephesus, or Smyrna, he will almost certainly
obtain either direct information from them, on this
as well as other subjects, or they will put him in the
way of obtaining the information he requires.

A very pretty present for a lady, and one which
my lady friends tell me is always an acceptable one,
can readily be obtained at Athens, and sometimes at
Corfu as well as at Smyrna,—I allude to the Greek
embroidered jacket. It goes with almost anything
I am informed, and particularly well with light white
stuffs, or better still with white and gold. The little
embroidered caps, which one can sometimes buy to
go with them, look exceedingly pretty, and seem to
suit almost all complexions. I do not know any part
of the world where more charming souvenirs of this
description can be bought; moreover, pretty presents,
which are always to be found in these Eastern shops
or bazaars, will suit all purses. Some lovely little

white head-dresses cost only 3 francs a piece, while
complete costumes, when richly embroidered, reach
almost to any figure ; if to these are added the silver
or gold belts recommended to be worn with the dress,
about as rich a present as can be purchased anywhere
may be secured. The shops, however, in which
you buy these jackets are not the best for the belts,
which can only be got really good from the jewellers.
Of the time it takes to purchase any article in the
East, I only wish I had one encouraging word to say.
If you desire to buy such a costume as I have
described, and you get it in three days, at anything
less than double its real value, you will have done
well. By far the best way in Smyrna, for instance, or
in the Jew's quarter in Corfu, is to *select* for yourself
and *get some resident to buy* for you ; if you buy it
yourself the odds are very long against you. These
Jewish, Armenian, or Greek merchants are wonderful
judges of men and women and their ways. The
weaker side of human nature is their special study,
and time is no object to them. You must, indeed,
go to work with a wonderful amount of self con-
fidence, if you think you are to get the best of
the bargain with any of these gentry. If, however,
for any reason you wish to deal directly (and I know
a lady who always does this, and with astonishing
success) then remember you have one advantage,
I think your only one. These vendors are very
jealous of each other, and, by a very small purchase
in another shop, you may succeed in bringing your
extortioner to reason. I learnt this from my lady
friend. We men are but poor creatures when it

comes to dealing. I honestly believe that if you make up your mind, in any of these localities, to spend say £20 in buying things, that a clever resident lady can, if she likes, give you double the value you could get otherwise for that sum. If you mean to spend £200, then she would save you even a larger proportion, as those articles which are only bought by rich people are heavily charged for, especially by Armenians; you will find that this is true in Smyrna more particularly. In Constantinople, frequent fires have all but destroyed those splendid old bazaars, so do not put off buying till you get there, as your choice of what may be called Eastern goods, is much smaller there than at Smyrna, or even at Athens. It is worth the yachtsman's while, also, to bear in mind the fact that, if time is generally on the side of the bazaar stall holder, it is a little also on his, as he may be calling at the same ports, or at least some of them, on his way home. This is necessarily true about Athens. As to the purchase of goods, not essentially Eastern, in Constantinople, I might as well write about going shopping in Paris.

In reference to sending home goods, perhaps I may be allowed to offer a hint which may be of use. If the purchaser should wish to send goods home by rail, it is well to bear in mind that, it is by no means an uncommon occurrence for trains to be blocked on the lines by snow during the winter. This was not unfrequently the case during the winter of 1895—96. The luggage and goods are naturally the last things to be thought of, the lives of the passengers and the mail being, of course, the first care of the Company. I can leave my reader to imagine what would happen, for example, to a Greek embroidered dress, if left in the snow for a few hours. Of course, when there is no hurry, the yacht herself could bring home anything, but I am supposing, for some reason or another, that this course is not desired. By inquiry at Cook's office, or of the British Consul or Vice-Consul, it is not difficult to ascertain what steamers are going either direct home or to Marseilles. There is almost always some shipping firm which will undertake delivery. This is the course I adopt myself in an ordinary way. If, however, I get a chance of seeing a home going Captain or purser myself, or, better still, the ship's steward (should she be a passenger steamer), I prefer a private arrangement, if love or money can secure it. Now and then exceptional facilities offer, as, for instance, the Consul is going home on leave, and you are his friend; or one of the Embassy or Legation staff. But, naturally, as a means of transport, this is not open to the general public. I should not have mentioned these facilities at all, had it not been that it affords me an opportunity of drawing attention to the uniform courtesy which yachtsmen in the East receive at the hands of the Diplomatic and Consular Staff, wherever they happen to call.

As I am on the question of transport, may I call attention to a dreadful Eastern practice, which is more common than is generally believed. Letters are treated with habitual neglect, in almost all Eastern post offices. If the letters you send home, and which are sent out to you, do *all* of them arrive

I

anyhow, whether punctually or not, you will have experienced what very few of your fellow travellers have done. But what is more trying still, is that, after taking all the precaution you can, if telegrams are sent to you through the post office, you often do not get them for hours, sometimes days, after their arrival. The Greeks, in this respect, are, I fancy, much greater sinners than the Turks. I will give one instance out of many. I sent from Syra, a wire to my friend, Mr. Maxse, the British Consul at the Piræus. The distance, as every one knows, is not great, and the telegraph line quite direct. It was a wire of great importance, both to me and to him. It was kept a whole day at the post office at the Piræus. On asking for an explanation, he was informed that the post offices authorities had been very busy on that particular day. I could tell many queer stories about the Postal Authorities, but, I think I have given, in this example, an idea of what travellers may expect as regards telegrams. I will give one as regards letters. I expected one of importance; it did not arrive, though it was due, and, after waiting three days, I went to sea. Six weeks later I arrived in England, and one week *after that* my letter arrived. I think I have fairly made out my case. Improvement, I am told, is going forward in this department, well, let us hope so, there is room.

I have now, I think, given all the general information in my power, in regard to our yachting route to Constantinople, its pros and its cons. There have been, perhaps, more cons than pros, yet I should be

GENERAL VIEW OF POROS.

sorry if, in anything I have written, I have dissuaded anyone from voyaging Eastward. Circumstances necessitated my going to Constantinople at the worst possible time of the year, and I shall have written to little purpose, if I have not made it clear that December, January, and February, are the least desirable months to select for seeing Stamboul, and for yachting in the East of the Mediterranean, the Ægean Sea, and Sea of Marmora.

I have recently been asked, by a lady who has much experience in yachting matters, and is herself an owner, what I should advise as regards a yachting trip to the East? And the answer I made her I have no reason to modify. I gave her a sketch of all the ports I visited on the road to Constantinople and back, and I think they will be found the most convenient; I then added, "do not go when I did." If you can get to Constantinople by October 15th, then go; you can then be back again to Corfu, or to the West of the Gulf of Corinth, amongst some well sheltered ports, before November 28th. If you cannot do this, then put off Constantinople till March 15th, and be back in the Mediterranean by May 1st. I hardly know whether this advice can be bettered. As far as my knowledge goes, and, as far as I can gather from others, I do not think I could improve on those dates.

It will be obvious to my readers, that the Gulf of Salonica, Mount Athos, and other places of great interest, have not been visited by me, but the omission will, I hope, suggest to others, more able than myself, the desirability of giving information and,

above all things, producing and publishing photos of
these and other places, along the North Coast of
these Eastern waters. So far as I am aware, no such
attempt has yet been made. The games at Athens,
the ever present Eastern question, and other incidents,
are all tending to turn the public eye in a direction,
where accurate information and accurate pictures will
be increasingly welcome. I am divulging no secret
between my publishers and myself, when I say that
they are quite prepared for any good book on this
subject. My own powers are far too limited, as well
as my opportunities; I cannot do more than to act
as a pioneer in a very humble manner, but the
reception the public and my critics were kind enough
to give my last work, has encouraged me, and
should encourage others. There is a heap of overwhelmingly interesting work to be done in the
Mediterranean, indeed, as one goes on, one sees how
much. If only a quarter of our yachting community
would give photos of the places at which they
anchor, and short descriptions, we should soon be
rich enough in knowledge. I am quite aware of
how much has been done.

Messrs. Cassell have published a most beautiful
work ("Picturesque Mediterranean"), and the wood-
cuts, engravings, and letterpress are all beyond praise,
but the book is large and, though a marvel of cheap-
ness as regards value given, it costs a good round
sum. This is not at all the sort of book I am
thinking of. The work that is wanted should be one
which would be at once smaller, handier, and
cheaper. It must, also, contain some *uninteresting*

GREEK MONASTERY, ON POROS ISLAND.

15

looking photos (of course I mean to the general public), and would have to run the gauntlet of the critics, in consequence. No human powers can make the entrance of many ports look interesting to the reading world in general, yet it is precisely these uninteresting looking places, the entrances to which are so difficult to recognize at a distance, which the navigator and the visitor most want. "Where is our harbour?" is the question on every one's lips when land is first sighted. A photograph of the entrance soon sets the enquirer at rest. Yet look at this photo by your fireside at home, and it seems the most uninteresting of pictures. Happily, this is not always the case, and the picturesque as well as the useful can often be combined.

May I here be permitted to mention a few works, which are much needed by all tourists in Eastern waters. No one half realizes the charm of the East, without a knowledge of both the Iliad and the Odyssey. Yet neither of these have been illustrated as they should be, with the places mentioned as they look now, and as they probably looked then, side by side. The interest of such a book would be enormous, and, if undertaken by a scholar, a draughts-man, and a photographer, would be of great and lasting value. The Bible ports, and places of interest, have been much more thought of and worked at, but a yachtsman's Bible, by which, I mean, a Bible full of photographs of the Bible ports, with hints at the bottom of each page as to the possibility of anchoring at places mentioned, is much wanted. The foot notes might also contain information as to the depth of the water, the leading marks, the best times of the year to go to these places, the prevailing winds, the possibility of getting pilots, and the prices to pay them ; water and coal supply up to date, together with interesting facts, in regard to ancient monuments or hieroglyphics, bearing on Bible history or Bible questions. I am quite aware of the opposition I may meet with, from those who would object to binding secular information within the covers of the sacred volume, but would not the gain be greater than the loss? No man writes a book without laying himself open to some criticism, and, in drawing attention to what seems to me a pressing want of Eastern tourists and yachtsmen, I must run some risk. I believe the cause to be a good one.

Now for another want. There would, at first sight, be something comical about the appearance of a book which might be called "The Yachtsman's History of Greece," for some cynic would be sure to suggest that the time seems to have arrived when yachtsmen, like children, must have their own History of Greece, and quite full of pictures. To which I should feel inclined to reply: "You enjoy the laugh, but let me enjoy the book." There is, as far as I am aware, no such work. Every yachtsman and tourist probably knows the names of the principal battles of ancient Greece, but very few indeed know the best anchorages, at different seasons of the year, to go to, in order to visit the sites where these took place. Photographs of these anchorages, as well as the battle-fields, as they now appear, might be interesting to a very wide circle of readers. Of

OUR CHIEF BEATER.

course, if you like to anchor in the Piræus, and send
your vessel over periodically to Poros for water, you
can visit every spot, by road or rail; some, for want
of good information, have already done so, or something like it. But this is not business. It is no use
having a home always with you wherever you go
(the yachtsman's splendid privilege), if you are de-
liberately to leave your comforts out of reach. An
instinct here tells me, that if I go on in this strain,
I shall get troublesome to my readers, so I shall
stop, and at once.

I have purposely left to the last the question of
scenery in Eastern waters. There is so much to read
in these days, that some tired souls may not im-
probably do with my book what they have done
with others, viz., read a bit here and there, then skip
on to the end. My finish, therefore, shall be an
answer to the question, "What is there to see?"
This is an important question. "Fancy yachting
with uninteresting scenery always. Who, then,
would ever buy a vessel at all?" Well, in your
Eastern travels you will not find this. No, a
thousand times no, though, at times, I felt myself
disappointed. But then I went at the worst time of
the year; yes, the very worst, for if I had gone in
July, I might have suffered much from the heat, but,
oh! those mornings and evenings! They are, I
know, worth more than can be described. How do
I know, as I was not there? Well, I have a lady
friend, whose more than beautiful sketches and
oil paintings have shown me what those lovely
Greek islands are like during the summer months.

120

Then she has a husband, about the best amateur photographer that I have ever known, and this artistic pair have many times and oft described the beauties surrounding their home during the warm season. "Now name your friends," says my reader.—No, I will not, but they live within a 100 miles of the Piræus. Nearer than this I will not go, except to say that the lady was once the favourite pupil of the greatest of French painting masters, and that she has exhibited in the Paris Salon. So you may work out the puzzle for yourself, then, if she exhibits again, you may buy her pictures. Consols now stand at 113; this picture investment will pay you better.

To return, I think the scenery North of the Piræus and the Greek Islands only beautiful here and there. There are many islands almost bare of trees; the Government has not encouraged, and the inhabitants have not had the enterprise, to replant those that have been cut down for fire-wood or destroyed by gales. But others there are that, during the best part of the year, must be beautiful. I will mention a few :—Poros, Mitylene, Syra, Patmos, Samos. The Island of Delos, though interesting as the birthplace of Apollo and Artemis, and the ruined temples once erected to their honour, can never be beautiful ; the lack of trees being only too conspicuous.

The passage of the Dardanelles, as every one knows, cannot be made at night, so all passengers are sure to see that most interesting locality. That is certainly always lovely, except when the snow is on the ground, when it looks about as dreary as it

is possible for any place to look. On both sides of
the Sea of Marmora the scenery is most lovely,
while its many islands add immensely to its beauty.
The state of the country is, however, so unsatisfactory,
that I should be sorry to form one of a sketching or
photographic party, unless I was very distinctly
within a sight of my vessel, and I had a boat handy
to take me on board. A large number of anchorages on both sides of the Sea of Marmora, however,
make sketching from the yacht comparatively easy,
while the entrance to the Bosphorus, when the
sun or, better still, the moon, is shining on Constantinople, with its many domes and minarets, has
too often attracted the artist for me to dwell at
length on the beauty of the scene. Unfortunately,
the smoke from the many steamers which ply up
and down the Bosphorus, makes all photographic
work unusually difficult, there being only a few, if
any, opportunities of getting satisfactory pictures
during the day. There are some beautiful bits of
scenery meeting the eye of the tourist, as he approaches the entrance to the Black Sea, and the
valley extending to Therapia is quite unquestionably
one of the prettiest of the many lovely valleys of
which Turkey can boast. On the homeward bound
journey, should there be time, I doubt if much more
attractive scenery can be found, than the view which
will present itself to the yachtsman's eye, if he can
resist the temptation of entering the harbour of
Vathy in Ithaca, and will steer between this island
and the island of Cephalonia. It is a very far cry,
indeed, from the Bosphorus to Ithaca, but I have

purposely drawn attention to these two places together, because of a very strange similarity of view when passing between Europe and Asia in one case, and the two islands mentioned in the other. Of course there are no palaces in the islands, but the configuration of the land, in both cases, is curiously similar. Both, certainly, are equally lovely. When passing Ithaca, the photographer and the artist can work without the drawback of smoky steamers, and, despite the popularity of the Bosphorus as a scene for artistic labour, I believe the Cephalonia channel will give even greater satisfaction to the worker.

I must now bid adieu to my reader, and must leave him to find out yet new beauties and new attractions for himself. There are plenty of these in these Eastern waters. I have only indicated, to those who have followed our cruise on paper, a few attractions and interests as they appeared to the writer, and to those who did him the honour to accompany him as his guests and companions. There is plenty of overwhelmingly interesting work to be done here, by any one who cares to give the public the result of his experiences, and will show also, by photographs, the many points of interest left untouched in this little work. If I have, in any degree, succeeded in re-awakening an interest in Grecian and Turkish waters, I shall feel more than repaid.

THE END.

APPENDIX.

THE following very admirable account of the opening of the Olympic Games, was published in the *Field* newspaper, of April 18th, 1896 :—

"The visitor to Athens now enters by the new underground railway, that terminates near the Place de la Concorde, so that he avoids the former long drive up the Ru du Stade, which is brilliantly decorated with flags of all kinds and colours, the Greek pale blue and white, of course, predominating. He soon sees that the whole city is en fête, and that nothing has been spared to show it at its best. The streets are thronged with strangers, for the most part Greeks from the provinces and islands, and adjacent shores of the Ægean and Levant, all attracted by the great athletic gathering, organized on a scale unapproached since classical times. The day fixed for the opening of the games was Easter Monday, which, this year, coincides with the anniversary of the Declaration of Independence, the Greek National Festival, April 6th. The games were to begin at 3 p.m., but, as early as 1 o'clock, people began to stream down towards the Stadium. By 2, there were vast groups every here and there, but they appeared as nothing in the vast edifice. All round the outside of the top the people were crowded, covering, also, the elevations on either flank of the building. Officers were stationed at all points of the Stadium, directing people to their places, and, in this respect, the arrangements were perfect, which is more than can be said of the facilities—or want of facilities—for members of the press, or of the telegraph and number board. All the seats in the lower half of the Stadium had cushions, stuffed with cotton wool. At 2.30, Mr. Deliyannis, the Prime Minister, appeared, and was cordially received. The stream of people continued to pour in till 3 o'clock. Soon afterwards, the King and Queen and Royal party entered, amid the acclamations of the multitude, and proceeded to their seats, to the strains of the national air. Then the Crown Prince, as President of the Games Committee, advanced, and read an address from the Committee to their Sovereign, congratulating him on the happy event. Then followed the Olympic Hymn, written by C. Palamas, and composed by the well-known Greek composer, Samaras, who led the massed bands and choirs, a splendid and thrilling piece of music, admirably rendered. The sight of the immense mass of people, in and around one building, was one never to be forgotten. It has been estimated that there were 40,000 people inside the Stadium, and almost as many round the outside.

In the evening, there were illuminations in the chief squares and streets of the city. The Rue du Stade, which runs from the Place de la Constitution to the Place de la Concorde, was lit up by arches of gas jets, stretching across from lamp-posts on opposite sides, at about every 40 paces, the effect, though produced by simple means, being very pretty. The squares, above mentioned, were lit up in the same way, the lamp-posts being also joined by garlands of green leaves. Bands of music, with torch-bearers, promenaded the streets."

I have been tempted to give the foregoing quotations in *extenso*, as being the best inducement which could be offered to yachtsmen to visit this interesting sight.* I must now add a few words of my own. There was a scheme, which was very favourably received by the Authorities in the Piræus, a few years ago, for extending their harbour accommodation. Every visitor to this port must have been struck by the very limited space which can be allotted to trading vessels and yachts in this harbour, when there are also in it several men-of-war. The scheme then proposed was, to run a breakwater across the entrance of the outer or quarantine harbour, and so enclose a sheet of water, which would nearly double the present accommodation for shipping. A quarantine harbour could, possibly, then be made in the Gulf of Salamis. This scheme was, for the moment, placed on the shelf, owing to a want of funds. Once

---

* The games are to be repeated annually ; so, at least, it is reported.

again, this excellent plan has come to the front, and there seems some chance of its being realized. Every yachtsman who, by his influence, can help forward this idea, will be doing a service, not only to the trading and yachting community generally, but to the Piræus, Athens, and, indeed, to the whole Greek nation. With the double attraction, not only of the Gulf of Corinth Canal and a really splendid harbour at the Piræus, such as, indeed, might and could be offered, not only would almost every Mediterranean yacht tending Eastward be attracted, but the path of the tourist would be made much more simple and easier than it is now. For a very small expenditure in money, considering the advantages, this improvement might be carried out.

The London Stereoscopic & Photographic Company, Limited, Printers, 54, Cheapside, E.C.

INDEX.

WITH THE YACHT, CAMERA, & CYCLE IN THE MEDITERRANEAN,

By EARL OF CAVAN, K.P.

SAMPSON LOW, MARSTON AND COMPANY.

OPINIONS OF THE PRESS.

"To yachtsmen and cyclists the volume should prove very useful and attractive, being full of practical information very pleasantly conveyed. The idea of employing the camera for the guidance of the yachtsman is an excellent one, and the result is so full of attraction, that even stay-at-home readers will find a great deal to interest them in the book. The views given of the Corinth Canal are very striking, and those of Bizerta are not less full of instruction and interest than Lord Cavan's enthusiastic verbal description of that remarkable harbour. Lord Cavan promises to continue and complete his work by obtaining photographs and giving information in reference to ports which he has not hitherto visited, should the present instalment prove acceptable. We have little doubt that this condition will be abundantly fulfilled. Nothing can be more delightful than a winter cruise in the Mediterranean to those who are fortunate enough to be able to enjoy it, and few yachtsmen contemplating such a cruise, are likely to regard their equipment as complete without a copy of Lord Cavan's useful little volume."—*Times.*

"The modern yachtsman is not contented with his ship; he also takes his camera to record his impressions, and his bicycle to enjoy a run on shore whenever he finds a good road near some port, and to astonish the natives who have never yet seen men and women spinning along balanced on wheels. All these things the Earl of Cavan and his party did, and their doings are set forth in a pleasantly written little volume, which is rendered a really valuable addition to the library of a yacht by the excellent photographs taken by a lady of the party. Most photographs of foreign places show the towns and harbours as the appear from the shore, but these pictures show them as they appear from the sea, a very different thing. As a rule the plates are very good, and those who know the places photographed, will recognise with pleasure the pictures they themselves would have taken had they only had a camera with them. It was a most enviable voyage, and Lord Cavan's book is full of useful hints for yachtsmen who intend to follow in his path. For those who stay at home, the little book with its wealth of illustrations is pleasant reading, while for those who go yachting in the Mediterranean, whether in their own boats or in co-operative steamships, it is an indispensable part of the library."—*Graphic.*

"Lord Cavan's exhilarating book affords abundant evidence of the wisdom of his recommendation. Many a pleasant bicycling tour will here be found associated with the experiences of life aboard ship, and the visits to the numerous spots around the Mediterranean that have so materially helped to furnish subjects for the extensive and pretty series of views reproduced by the photomezzotype process, by the London Stereoscopic and Photographic Company, which are the especial glory of the volume. Not to every man's lot does it fall to go to Corinth, says the Latin poet; and yacht cruises in the Mediterranean are unhappily not within the reach of all; but the reader will get from these pages, with their endless accompaniment of sun pictures, a very fair notion of the yachtsman's peculiar sense of freedom and keen enjoyment of the ever-moving panorama of sea and shore."—*Daily News.*

"A volume useful alike to the ordinary tourist, the yachtsman, and the cyclist, for its author has carefully culled information for each. But its pictures give the work its chief value—nearly a hundred excellent full-page photogravures from prints taken under the direct supervision of the Earl, and giving a splendid idea of the many ports and places which his party visited."—*Review of Reviews.*

"Is an altogether admirable record of yachting and shooting in the Mediterranean and thereabouts. It contains close upon a hundred full-page photographs, and cannot but please the reader, whether it does or does not produce its effect by awakening in him pleasant memories of past journeys in the same blue water and romantic islands." —*Black and White.*

"A pleasant, gossipy narrative, written evidently with a view to the benefit of other travellers over the same route."—*Bookman.*

"The book is, in fact, a chatty and sumptuously illustrated supplement to the 'Mediterranean Pilot,' with hints thrown in for the benefit of those who are photographers and bicyclists as well as yachtsmen, one of the chief objects of the author being to provide the navigator with pictures of the approaches of the various harbours, to assist him in recognizing and entering them. In a subsequent volume he hopes to deal in the same way with the harbours of the Levant and the Archipelago, the particular cruise of which the present book is mainly a description not extending further eastward than Athens."—*Pall Mall Gazette.*

"More than a hundred full-page illustrations, from photographs excellently reproduced by the Stereoscopic Company, space out a fair-sized volume, which contains less than as many pages of letterpress. These photographs are certainly the principal feature of the book. And since one object of Lord Cavan's account of his Mediterranean yachting tours, with the bicycle on board for inland excursions, was to give the reader a real notion of what the principal Mediterranean ports are like, he may be said to have done his very best in this direction. For cycling, Lord Cavan speaks of the South of France as a paradise. If you go to Spain, leave your own bicycle at home and hire one on the spot ; the roads are bad and the Custom House worse. Without being in any way pretentious, this book is pleasantly written and pretty withal."—*St. James's Gazette.*

"To some ninety pages of letterpress there are about one hundred pages of illustrations, in what is called photomezzotype, and these are of unusual excellence. They are from photographs by Miss Olive Holdsworth, who was one of the party on a yachting expedition extending to Algeria, Sicily, the Ionian Islands, Greece, and most other parts of the Mediterranean coast that are best worth visiting. The points of view are skilfully chosen, and the result is to produce works of art of a standard very different from that attained by most amateurs. It would be difficult to improve such pictures as those of 'Sunset over the town of Corinth,' and of the Harbour of Ponza, and as most of them have been taken from the sea, they will furnish yachtsmen with a useful means of identifying various out-of-the-way places. Lord Cavan's hints, too, will be of substantial value to those who are inclined to follow his course, and he takes care to note where provisions, water, and coal may be best obtained, and what ports are convenient centres for inland exploration and supply roads suited to bicycles. Some of the practical hints to navigators are very useful, as, for example, the warning that at one place outside Bizerta, where the chart marks seven fathoms, the actual depth is only four and a half fathoms."—*Morning Post.*

"The illustrations are so numerous that, to a certain extent, this book may be regarded as an album with descriptive letterpress ; but in addition to this the author gives some valuable information to navigators, the outlines of two cruises in the Mediterranean, a good deal of information that will be useful to cyclists, and concludes with some general hints to yachtsmen and yacht builders. The book is very well got up, it is written in a pleasant, readable style, and the illustrations, which have been produced in photomezzotype by the London Stereoscopic and Photographic Company, are worthy of special commendation."—*Field.*

"The small volume before us contains a short but pleasantly-written account of the cruise, and is illustrated with nearly one hundred photographs, taken by Miss Holdsworth, one of the party, and printed by The London Stereoscopic Company. The object of the Earl, who is himself an experienced yachtsman, has been firstly to supply a series of photographs which will give some idea of the appearance of the ports, &c., to an approaching visitor; to indicate some of the principal objects of interest in each locality, and to furnish information, supplementary to that contained in the ordinary guide-books and manuals, which will be serviceable to yachtsmen and cyclists. There is no doubt that intending visitors to the countries described might derive many useful hints from this work, the small size of which renders it sufficiently portable to be used as a companion to the guide-books. The illustrations are excellent; and we observe with pleasure that the author hopes to follow up the present volume with others at a later date, illustrating parts of the Mediterranean not visited during his last cruise."—*The Spectator.*

"It is rarely that a volume of travel-talk about more or less familiar places is as charming as is the Earl of Cavan's little volume. The book is written in a bright, pleasing, and informing manner, and is enriched with close upon one hundred full-page plates from photographs, illustrating all the more important places visited. Not only does the author describe his own journeyings, but he gives his readers the benefit of his experience in mapping out some suggested tours, and in giving some hints to yachtsmen in the Mediterranean. To visit the Mediterranean is a strong desire with most people; an hour spent with this delightful volume will not only add considerably to their knowledge of Southern Europe, but will even further accentuate the desire to be off on a prolonged trip to those sunny scenes."—*Publisher's Circular.*

"The cream of travelling for pleasure is still that which is to be found on the shores of the Mediterranean, and the most delightful of all means of visiting the famous cities and beautiful scenes fringing the Middle Sea is that provided by a well-bound, comfortable, and seaworthy yacht. But if we may credit the Earl of Cavan, a yacht is not rightly equipped unless she have a camera and bicycle on board. With the one the voyager, or, as on board the 'Roseneath,' some fair member of the party detailed for the duty, snaps impressions by the way to pleasure and profit after days and other travellers. With the other, an amount of freedom and ease of locomotion on land is obtained rivalling that which the yacht provides at sea. The photographs taken by Miss O. Holdsworth, and printed in photomezzotype by the London Stereoscopic Company are undoubtedly the great feature of Lord Cavan's 'With the Yacht, Camera, and Cycle.' To stay-at-home people they bring a gust of Mediterranean lands and seas that will infallibly kindle the desire to see with their own eyes the places visited by the 'Roseneath's' party. To others accustomed to yacht cruising, they will be of real service as well as pleasure, by supplementing in a way that only photographic art can do, the information given concerning harbour entrances and the like by such duller media as the guide-books and the Admiralty charts. Lord Cavan's running log of the cruise is just such a bright, unassuming, and useful narrative of the ground gone over, as yachtsmen will wish to possess. It is thoroughly practical in its spirit; and description and counsel are thoroughly good of their kind. Yachting has never been placed in a more attractive light before the world than in this little volume, which the author has dedicated to the Prince of Wales."—*Scotsman.*

"We have nothing but praise for this book, and can cordially recommend it to any one who is projecting a winter tour in the Mediterranean. It is, perhaps, the most unsentimental journey that we have ever read, and, considering the object with which it is written, one of the best. Lord Cavan, in fact, discards all the usual methods of the writers of travels, carefully avoids boring the reader with needless detail or irrelevant description, and presents him instead with plenty of practical advice and with a series of photographs, of which many will be found useful as well as beautiful. So far from padding his little book—for it is quite short—Lord Cavan surprises one by the quantity of plain information that he has packed into a small compass. He cruised in a schooner yacht of two hundred tons, with auxiliary steam-power, from Gibraltar to Athens, paying off the yacht at Leghorn on the return journey. He carried bicycles for himself and for some of the ladies of the party, and recommends every one to do the same ; and more, he is careful to note the condition of the roads wherever he went, and the facilities for the repair or the hire of machines. This, indeed, is one of his objects in writing the book, now that all the world goes on wheels. Another of Lord Cavan's objects, as a practical yachtsman, was to give, by means of photographs, an idea of the appearance of the various ports from the offing. As he truly says, every navigator will appreciate a picture of the port he is about to visit. His information is short and useful, and he hardly ever departs from the businesslike character he has assumed, though his pages are now and then lightened agreeably by such events as the shooting of a wild boar, or the bribing, with instantaneous effect, of a magnificent Spanish customs official. Having said this much of what Lord Cavan modestly calls 'the letterpress,' we must briefly express our admiration of the many excellent photographs or heliographs that adorn the book. We infer, from internal evidence, that they are the work of Miss Olive Holdsworth, one of Lady E. Lambart's friends and companions. They have been done with equal skill and intelligence, and it is no exaggeration to say that they leave nothing to be desired."—*National Observer*.

"Not everybody can go cruising in the Mediterranean, but those who can will find in the Earl of Cavan's 'With the Yacht, Camera, and Cycle in the Mediterranean' many hints and much information, and those who cannot will at least enjoy the reading of the book. It is to be hoped that the Earl's attempt to supply a sort of unconventional handbook to the Mediterranean will encourage him to make, as is his intention, another, and give photographs of and information concerning the Mediterranean ports which he has not hitherto visited."—*Westminster Gazette*.

"In Lord Cavan's addition to the guide-books of the Mediterranean, the camera results quite dwarf the author's descriptions of yachting and cycling, there being in it a larger number of full-page photos than pages of letterpress. The illustrations are, however, so well done and excellently reproduced that they alone make the book valuable, and one of the chief intentions of the work—namely, to show yachtsmen the appearance of the Mediterranean ports from the sea at varying distances—is very well carried out. The volume is full of useful hints to yachtsmen as to anchorages and other practical matters ; and to cyclists, regarding the landing of machines, possibilites of hiring, roads, and so on."—*World.*